THE VERY SCARY ALMANAC

BY ERIC ELFMAN

ILLUSTRATIONS BY WILL SUCKOW

RANDOM HOUSE   NEW YORK

For Jan, who, late at night,
while I was working on the scariest parts
of this book, took great delight in sneaking up
behind me and shouting "Boo!"
—E. E.

Copyright © 1993 by RGA Publishing Group, Inc.
All rights reserved under International and Pan-American
Copyright Conventions. Published in the United States by
Random House, Inc., New York, and simultaneously in
Canada by Random House of Canada Limited, Toronto.

Library of Congress Cataloging-in-Publication Data

Elfman, Eric.
The very scary almanac / by Eric Elfman; illustrations by Will Suckow.
   p.   cm.
Published simultaneously in Canada.
Includes bibliographical references.
Summary: An almanac of facts about witchcraft, ghosts, vampires,
zombies, horror movies, superstitions, and other scary subjects.
ISBN 0-679-84401-5 (pbk.)
1. Occultism—Juvenile literature. 2. Occultism—Terminology—
Juvenile literature. 3. Parapsychology—Juvenile literature. 4.
Fear—Miscellanea—Juvenile literature. [1. Supernatural.]
I. Suckow, Will, ill. II. Title.
BF1411.E37 1993
133—dc20

Manufactured in the United States of America 0 9 8 7 6 5 4 3 2 1

CONTENTS

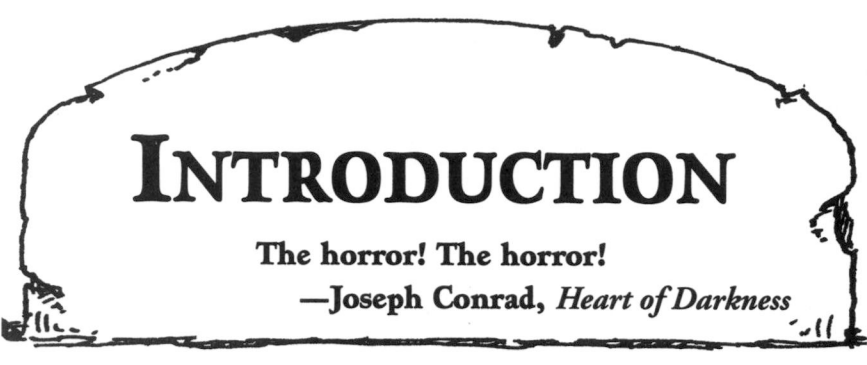

INTRODUCTION

The horror! The horror!
—Joseph Conrad, *Heart of Darkness*

A high-school girl is baby-sitting when suddenly all the lights in the house flicker out. Is it a blown fuse? The girl gropes around for a flashlight and heads down the cobwebby cellar stairs to the fuse box. But there's nothing the matter with the fuses. She switches them on and off. The fuses are fine. Someone has severed the line to the house! She breaks out in a sweat. Then she hears what sounds like the picnic table on the back patio being dragged across the cement. And the creak of the kitchen window being opened.

Finally she hears the shuffle and thud of someone stepping onto the kitchen table and jumping to the floor. She hears a snuffling sound, a growl. The door from the kitchen opens. She's afraid to look, but she has to, and what she sees standing at the top of the stairs makes her blood run cold and freezes the scream in her throat.

There's nothing funny about this scene. But we pay lots of money to see ones just like it in movies every day. Why do we do it? What is it about horror that's so intoxicating? Could it be that, maybe, being afraid is *fun*? Think about it. That tingling sensation running from the base of your neck down your spine can really be quite pleasant. It's thrilling to think that ghosts and spirits and demons are real. Stretching your imagination is more exciting than stretching your legs. It's fun to imagine that the worst may happen, especially when you least expect it—envision a hideously rotting corpse appearing in the bathroom mirror as you brush your teeth!

People have always known fear. They have been scared of monsters, demons, witches, curses, and ghosts. Experts in the fields of folklore (the beliefs, customs, and stories shared by a

4

group of people) and anthropology (the study of humanity and the origins of our cultures) explain that ancient peoples invented these creatures as a way to deal with their fear of things they could not understand. The cause of a crop failure, they might imagine, was a demon out for revenge. A howling wind could be the shrieking voice of a murdered man seeking vengeance.

Of course, to be fair, it *is* possible that people believed (and often still do believe) in monsters, demons, witches, and ghosts because they saw them with their own eyes. Every culture throughout history has believed in one form of the supernatural or another. Is it just coincidence? Have people throughout the ages and around the globe just made up the same things? Or could it be that witches' spells really *can* work magic? That demons and monsters *are* lying in wait to pounce in the darkness? That villagers *have* watched werewolves attack travelers? That mourning relatives *have* seen loved ones return from the grave as zombies? We know all too well that madmen *do* roam the earth. Why not zombies, ghouls, and ghosts? Are they really any less far-out than the people who frequent our nightly news?

So lock the doors, turn on the lights, and settle in. But don't get too comfortable! You're going to read about the very scariest things in the world, and chances are you'll never feel quite as safe again.

CREEPY CULTURE

Every society, in every land, in every time, has had its own legends about monsters. These creeps date back as far as the Middle Ages and slither through history right up to the latest horror movie villain. Read on and discover the scariest characters, both past and present, of legend, book, and film.

MONSTERS, GHOULS & FEATURED CREATURES

Listen to them—the children of the night. What music they make!

—Bram Stoker, *Dracula*

Following is a catalog of the most loathsome monsters and terrifying creatures from around the world. Although many of them haven't been spotted in quite some time, there's always the possibility that they are lying in wait for some innocent victim.

THE BLOB: One of the most frightening monsters of horror movies, the Blob is a gooey, sticky mass from outer space that eats people by covering them completely and absorbing their bodies. It moves through pipes, oozing through

cracks and drains—no place or person is safe from the Blob! This gelatinous ghoul made its screen debut in the 1958 film *The Blob* and returned in a sequel, *Beware! The Blob,* in 1972.

FRANKENSTEIN'S MONSTER: Made of the stitched-together body parts of corpses and brought to life by Victor Frankenstein, Frankenstein's monster is one of the most tragic characters of horror novels and films. Created by Mary Shelley in her book *Frankenstein* (written in 1818), the monster has only one desire: to be human—a desire that is never fulfilled. The monster is forced by an unsympathetic world to remain an outcast—and to seek revenge.

> By the glimmer of the half-extinguished light, I saw the dull yellow eye of the creature open; it breathed hard, and a convulsive motion agitated its limbs. . . . Great God! His yellow skin scarcely covered the work of muscles and arteries beneath; his hair was of a lustrous black, and flowing; his teeth of a pearly whiteness; but these luxuriances only formed a more horrid contrast with his watery eyes, that seemed almost of the same color as the dun white sockets in which they were set, his shriveled complexion, and straight black lips.
>
> —Mary Shelley, *Frankenstein*

GHOULS: Centuries ago, the people of western Europe believed that these ghastly creatures ate human corpses, especially enjoying the bodies of young children. Ghouls came to graveyards at night and pulled the dead from their graves. On occasion they ate living victims—especially those who interrupted them while they dined!

GODZILLA: A huge, cinematic dinosaur-type creation, Godzilla terrorized the Japanese countryside. After being awakened by underwater testing of the atomic bomb, Godzilla left Tokyo in ruins in its first film, produced in Japan in 1956. Since then it has destroyed the city again and again in countless sequels and remakes, including *King Kong vs. Godzilla* (1963), *Godzilla vs. the Thing* (1964), *Son of Godzilla* (1967), and *Godzilla's Revenge* (1969).

JINN: The ancient Arabic peoples believed in many types of jinn (the plural of genie). All are capable of magic, to a greater or lesser degree, and all are malicious (bad news):

- **Jann** are the lowest and weakest type of genie.
  - **Djinn** are the most common type, but still not very powerful, which is why they are often caught and imprisoned in bottles. They are reportedly very ugly (not at all like Barbara Eden in *I Dream of Jeannie*) and torment people just for the fun of it.
- **Shaitans** are more powerful than the djinn, more dangerous, and even uglier. They eat dirt and other waste. Like it or not, everybody has his or her own personal shaitan urging that person to do evil, along with a guardian angel urging the individual to do good.
- **Marida** are the most powerful jinn of all. They concern themselves only with tempting and tormenting kings, presidents, and other powerful people.

THE MUMMY: Fascination with the discovery of King Tut's tomb in 1922 led to the creation of this movie monster in the 1932 film *The Mummy*. A living mummy returns after thousands of years to fulfill a curse and to reclaim the reincarnated soul of the woman he loved.

VAMPIRES: A living corpse who must drink blood to survive, the vampire is one of the most popular creatures in all folklore. Legends of vampirelike creatures exist throughout the world and date from before written history. However, most of the modern myths and lore that are associated with vampires (such as the idea that a vampire cannot be seen in a mirror) originated in the legends of sixteenth-century eastern Europe.

HOW TO PROTECT YOURSELF FROM A VAMPIRE:

- While a vampire sleeps, place a wild rose on its coffin. The vampire will not be able to get out.

- Lay a broom on a vampire's grave, or scatter handfuls of grain on the ground. When the vampire comes out at night, it will be compelled to count the straws of the broom or the individual grains. If you use a big enough broom or enough grain, you can keep the vampire busy until sunrise.

- When being chased by a vampire, try to cross a bridge over a river. Vampires can't cross running water.

- Wear or hold a cross, a Christian symbol, to keep a vampire away.

- Wear garlands of garlic around your neck.

- Never invite a suspected vampire into your house. Vampires can't enter a home without being invited. But once they are asked in, they can come and go as they please.

Arthur took the stake and the hammer, and when once his mind was set on action his hands never trembled nor even quivered.... [He] placed the point over the heart.... Then he struck with all his might.

The Thing in the coffin writhed; and a hideous, blood-curdling screech came from the opened red lips. The body shook and quivered and twisted in wild contortions; the sharp white teeth champed together till the lips were cut, and the mouth was smeared with a crimson foam ... whilst the blood from the pierced heart welled and spurted up around it.

—Bram Stoker, *Dracula*

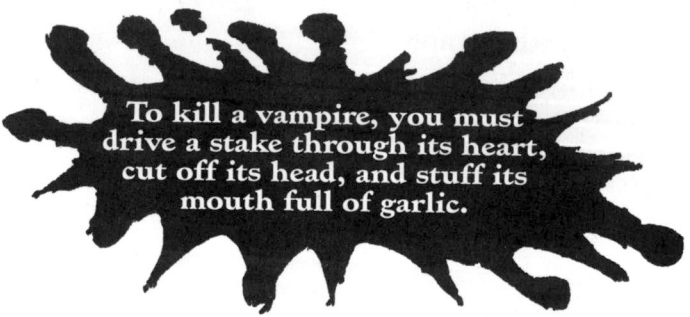

To kill a vampire, you must drive a stake through its heart, cut off its head, and stuff its mouth full of garlic.

WEREWOLVES: The existence of the werewolf, a person who can turn into a wolf, is one of the oldest and most widespread beliefs in the world of monsters. Details have varied in different places and times, but people from ancient to modern times have shared these beliefs about werewolves:

- The transformation happens at night. Some people believe that the moon must be full as well.

- When in its wolf form, a werewolf is ravenously hungry. It will attack and eat animals and sometimes people.

- When a werewolf has eaten its fill, it returns to its human form.

- If a werewolf is wounded or killed while in its wolf form, when it changes back into its human form it will likewise be injured or dead.

- The only way to become a werewolf is to be bitten by one.

ZOMBIES: In Haitian voodoo, a zombie is a dead body brought back to life by a bocor, a witch doctor or evil sorcerer. Zombies are mindless slaves, working endlessly doing whatever they are told. A zombie must be fed occasionally to keep it working, but it must never taste salt, for then it will remember that it is dead and will return to its grave to die again—this time for good.

> **TERRIFYING TIDBIT:** In Haiti, the fear of becoming one of these lifeless creatures is so great that there is a law that makes it a crime to turn someone into a zombie.

A bocor creates a zombie by walking to his victim's house backward. He sucks out the person's soul through an opening in the door, then quickly blows it into a bottle, which he seals immediately. Without a soul, the victim wastes away and dies. After the person is buried, the sorcerer goes to the grave and digs up the body. He speaks some spells over it, then returns the soul to the body. The sorcerer calls the person's name, and if the dead person answers, the sorcerer can bring the body back to life.

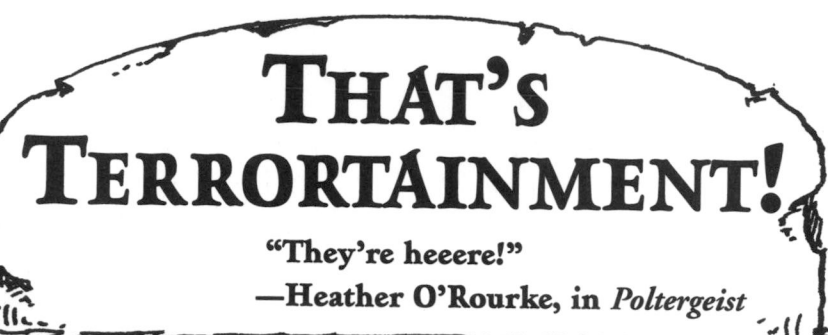

THAT'S TERRORTAINMENT!

"They're heeere!"
—Heather O'Rourke, in *Poltergeist*

Before recorded history, people gathered around the flickering light of the tribal fire to hear wise men tell stories of demons and monsters and the never-ending battle between good and evil. Thousands of years later, we still gather around flickering lights—those of TV sets and movie theaters—to be frightened out of our wits. Technology may have changed, but the stories of ghosts, witches, vampires, madmen, and monsters found on the screen and written page are not so different from the ones that terrified our ancestors.

GREAT MOMENTS IN HORROR LITERATURE

Want a good read? A book that will send chills down your spine and make you afraid to turn the page? According to critics and literary scholars, these are the twenty best horror novels and books of short stories ever written, arranged by date of publication. (Although some of them have parts that might be difficult to read, their downright scariness makes them worth a try!)

1818 — *Frankenstein*, by Mary Shelley. The classic story of a man-made monster.

1819 — *The Vampyre*, by Dr. John Polidori. The first vampire novel.

1820 — *Melmoth the Wanderer*, by Charles Maturin. A man sells his soul to the devil so he can live forever, and then decides he wants out of the deal.

1845 — *Tales*, by Edgar Allan Poe. A collection of scary short stories by the King of Creep.

1886 — *The Strange Case of Dr. Jekyll and Mr. Hyde*, by Robert Louis Stevenson. A mild-mannered doctor creates a potion that unleashes his dark side.

1891 — *The Picture of Dorian Gray*, by Oscar Wilde. The story of a man whose portrait gets older while he remains young.

1893 — *Can Such Things Be?* by Ambrose Bierce. A collection of chilling short stories.

Edgar Allan Poe (1809–1849)

Edgar Allan Poe's tragic life no doubt contributed to the terrifying horror found in his stories. His mother died when he was two. He was diagnosed as having a brain lesion in his twenties. He had trouble holding a job throughout his life, and he died at the age of forty. In his short life, however, he invented the mystery story as we know it and wrote volumes of poetry, including *The Raven and Other Poems* (1845), and dozens of short stories that are as scary today as when he wrote them.

1897 — *Dracula,* by Bram Stoker. The undisputed king of vampires.

1898 — *The War of the Worlds,* by H. G. Wells. Martians invade a defenseless earth.

1898 — *The Turn of the Screw,* by Henry James. A psychological ghost story.

1911 — *The Phantom of the Opera,* by Gaston Leroux. The tale of a mysterious figure who haunts the Paris Opera House.

1913 — *The Lodger,* by Mrs. Belloc Lowndes. The story of Jack the Ripper.

1915 — *The Golem,* by Gustav Meyrink. Based on an ancient Jewish legend, a creature made of clay and built to help people runs amok.

1942 — *The Uninvited,* by Dorothy Macardle. The uninvited guests of the title are ghosts.

1954 — *I Am Legend,* by Richard Matheson. A new take on the vampire story—everyone on earth, except for one man, becomes a vampire.

1959 — *The Haunting of Hill House,* by Shirley Jackson. The story of an ill-fated attempt to exorcise a haunted house.

1959 — *Psycho,* by Robert Bloch. The basis for Alfred Hitchcock's classic film about a psychotic killer.

1967 — *Rosemary's Baby,* by Ira Levin. A woman is tricked into having the Devil's child.

1971 — *The Exorcist,* by William Peter Blatty. The story of a little girl possessed by a demon, and the attempts to save her.

1975 — *Salem's Lot,* by Stephen King. The story of a town overrun by vampires.

. . . AND FIVE CLASSIC SCARY SHORT STORIES

1902 — "The Monkey's Paw," by W. W. Jacobs. After ninety years, it remains one of the scariest stories ever written. A hideous artifact allows the bearer three wishes—but they come true in unpredictable, disastrous ways.

1928 — "The Call of Cthulhu," by H. P. Lovecraft. This and many of his other short stories tell of a cult that worships the strange creature/god Cthulhu (pronounced "k'thoo-loo").

[It was] a monster, of a form which only a diseased fancy could conceive. If I say that my somewhat extravagant imagination yielded simultaneous pictures of an octopus, a dragon, and a human caricature, I shall not be unfaithful to the spirit of the thing: A pulpy, tentacled head surmounted a grotesque and scaly body with rudimentary wings.
—H. P. Lovecraft, "The Call of Cthulhu"

1933 — "The Rocking-Horse Winner," by D. H. Lawrence. An eerie story of ghosts and the supernatural.

1937 — "The Devil and Daniel Webster," by Stephen Vincent Benét. A lawyer has to defend his client before a jury of murderers, traitors, and madmen.

1949 — "The Lottery," by Shirley Jackson. Generally agreed upon by literary critics and scholars to be the most chilling horror story of the twentieth century. A must-read for all chill-seekers.

THE SCARIEST BOOKS EVER WRITTEN

What was the scariest book you ever read? It was probably a fictional story made up to scare kids. The following books are very different. These books don't tell stories; rather they inform the reader how to perform black magic or raise dark spirits, or they reveal the innermost secrets of a witch's coven. These books, which you may be able to find at a large library or occult bookstore, aren't scary in the same way that a Stephen King or Christopher Pike book is scary, but they are some of the scariest books ever written—because they claim to be true!

The Book of the Sacred Magic of Abra-Melin the Mage, 1458. This is one of the most famous books dealing with magic. Anyone who masters its secrets will possess the most potent magic possible—but it is not without its dangers: People have been known to burn their

> **TERRIFYING TIDBIT:**
> One magician studying *The Book of the Sacred Magic* carelessly marked his place with a bill from his butcher. The next day the butcher was cutting meat in his shop when his knife slipped. He cut himself and bled to death before anyone could save him.

fingers using it. Aleister Crowley, a famous occult magician, called it "the best and most dangerous book ever written."

***Malleus Maleficarum (The Hammer of the Witches)*,** by Jacob Sprenger and Heinrich Kramer, 1486. This book, written by two self-proclaimed "experts" on witches, was used for hundreds of years by witch-hunters trying to rid Europe of all witches. It describes how to find, put on trial, and destroy witches. This book appeared during the witch hysteria of the Middle Ages, and helped lead to the torture and murder of thousands of innocent men and women.

***Ritual of High Magic*,** by Eliphas Levi, 1856. This book describes how to perform conjuration (raising spirits). The author explains his beliefs about how and why magic works. Although many scholars of demonology called Levi's book "nonsense," it became very popular, and it still influences the way real magicians think about supernatural forces.

***Gospel of the Witches (or The Aradia)*,** 1899. A collection of rituals, spells, charms, and other magic, this book is used by many modern witchcraft covens (groups of witches who worship together). Every copy to be used by a witch must be written out by hand by the witch who is going to use it. These handwritten copies are kept very secret, and they are almost impossible for an outsider to see.

***The Book of Shadows*,** by Gerald Gardner and Aleister Crowley, 1940. Gerald Gardner, founder of a witchcraft cult in England, asked Aleister Crowley to write a book of rites and rituals for him. The result was a prayer book and instruction manual that is still used by all the covens of Gardner's cult.

> **Whenever you have need of anything . . . assemble in a secret place and adore Me who am Queen of all Witcheries. There shall you assemble, you who are eager to learn all sorcery. I shall teach you things unknown.**
>
> **—*The Book of Shadows***

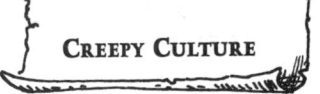

HOORAY FOR HORRORWOOD: THE CRITICS' PICKS

When story, mood, suspense, characters, and all-out chills
come together, you have a horror classic, one that will stand
the test of time. The following is a chronological list of the
horror movies that critics have chosen over the years as the
scream of the crop.

Nosferatu (1922)
Phantom of the Opera (1925)
Dracula (1931)
Frankenstein (1931)
Vampyr (1932)
King Kong (1933)
Bride of Frankenstein (1935)
Mad Love (1935)
I Walked with a Zombie (1943)
Beauty and the Beast (1946)
The Thing (1951)
The Night of the Hunter (1955)
Invasion of the Body Snatchers (1956)
Curse of the Demon (1958)
Psycho (1960)
The Pit and the Pendulum (1961)
Carnival of Souls (1962)
The Birds (1963)
The Night Stalker (1971)
Invasion of the Body Snatchers (remake, 1978)
Poltergeist (1982)

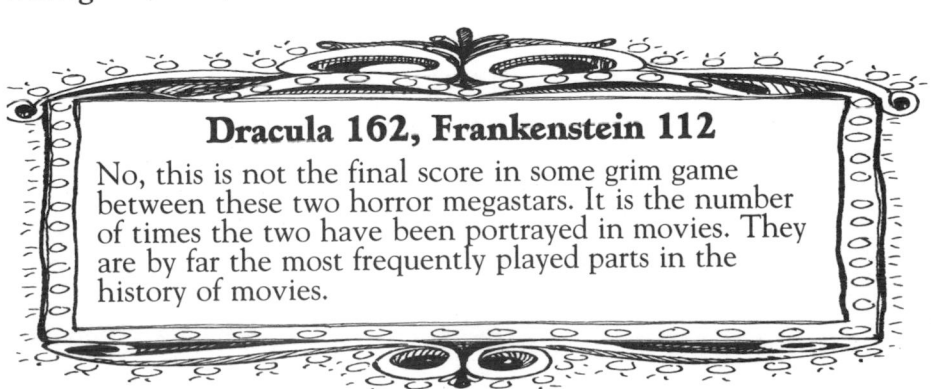

Dracula 162, Frankenstein 112

No, this is not the final score in some grim game
between these two horror megastars. It is the number
of times the two have been portrayed in movies. They
are by far the most frequently played parts in the
history of movies.

Top Grossers

Although not necessarily the scariest movies ever made, here are the fifteen biggest money-makers in the thriller and horror category.

Title	At the Box Office
Jaws (1975)	$ 129,549,000
Terminator 2 (1991)	$ 112,000,000
The Exorcist (1973)	$ 89,000,000
Bram Stoker's Dracula (1992)	$ 82,417,000
Gremlins (1984)	$ 79,500,000
Silence of the Lambs (1991)	$ 59,882,000
Jaws 2 (1978)	$ 50,431,000
Aliens (1986)	$ 43,700,000
Alien (1979)	$ 40,300,000
Poltergeist (1982)	$ 38,248,000
The Amityville Horror (1979)	$ 35,000,000
Arachnophobia (1990)	$ 31,366,000
Predator (1987)	$ 31,000,000
The Shining (1980)	$ 30,900,000
The Omen (1976)	$ 28,544,000

THE YEAR IN FEAR: A SCARY CALENDAR

**Trod beside me, close and dear,
The beautiful and death-struck year.**

—A. E. Housman, *A Shropshire Lad*

Mark your calendar—these are some of the scariest and most superstitious days of the year. Some of these days celebrate ancient, forgotten customs; others are still practiced today.

January 6: Epiphany

According to English tradition, brooms should be tied down on this day to prevent them from being used by witches. Throughout Europe, the dead are believed to walk on this night. In Austria, this is called St. Bertha's Night, when Austrians believe that the Devil is abroad in the land.

February 2: Candlemas

Try to avoid cemeteries on this day, because if you hear a bell toll at a funeral, the number of peals will equal the number of days that will pass before you hear of a friend's death.

February 18–20: Feralia, Feast of Manes

A Roman ceremony, the Feast of Manes honored the Manes—good spirits in charge of cemeteries. During the Feast of Manes, sacrifices of food were offered to these spirits, and the blood of black sheep, pigs, and oxen was poured over selected graves.

March 1

The English believe this is a very unlucky day to plant trees.

March 22: The Feast of Cybele

In this ancient Near Eastern agricultural/fertility festival, a pine tree was felled in the forest and dragged to the goddess Cybele's temple. There the trunk was treated like a corpse—wrapped in linen and mourned over. The festival culminated in the Day of Blood.

March 24: The Day of Blood

On the last day of the Feast of Cybele, a high priest drew blood from his arm and gave it as tribute to the goddess.

TERRIFYING TIDBIT: During the Day of Blood, all the townsmen played a role in worshiping their goddess. Then, those who were caught up in the excitement would cut off parts of their bodies and run through the city, throwing the parts into houses at random!

March 25: Kaous

In Greece it is believed that if a woman conceives on March 25 and gives birth on Christmas Eve, the child will become a Kaous—a malicious demon.

April 4: St. Mark's Day

According to an old English tradition, if you sit inside a church door on St. Mark's Eve at midnight, you will see the ghosts of all the townspeople who will die in the coming year pass into the church.

April 30: May Eve

In Ireland people believed that food left over from May Eve must not be eaten but rather buried, in order to avoid great harm.

Today on the Isle of Man, the youngest member of each family gathers primroses on this evening and throws them before the door of the family home to keep out evil spirits.

April 30: Walpurgis Night

Walpurgis Night is a huge festival for witches, especially in Germany. If you wear a piece of wild radish on this night, you will be able to see ghosts and witches. If you spot a hopping or grazing rabbit the next morning, it is actually a witch in disguise.

Be on the Lookout!
On the evening of Walpurgis Night, stick a thorn in your door so witches can't enter your house.

May 1: Beltaine (the "fire of god")
During this festival of the Druids, priests of the Celts, human sacrifices took place. Volunteers were placed inside a hollow statue of a god, which was then filled with twisted twigs and set on fire.

May 3: Dismal Day
The English believe it is unlucky to begin any new work or business on this day.

May 9, 11, 13: Lemuralia
According to ancient Roman superstition, these three days were used to rid one's home of lemures, evil spirits of the dead. During this time marriages and other happy events were prohibited. To get rid of the lemures, the Romans (with their faces turned away) threw black beans on the graves of the dead. They also burned black beans in their homes. They believed the stench would make the ghosts go away.

May 14: St. Boniface's Day
The Scottish believe that whatever day of the week St. Boniface's Day falls on will be an unlucky day throughout the rest of the year. (For example, if it falls on a Sunday, then *every* Sunday of the year will be unlucky!)

May 17: St. Dunstan's Day
According to English tradition, it is unlucky to be born on this day.

June 23: Summer Solstice
In Morocco, an offering of burning straw was made on this day to Qandisa, the Moroccan demon of rivers and springs.

July 25: St. James' Day

In Germany, it is considered very unlucky to climb a tree on St. James' Day.

August 1: Lammas Day

Lammas Day, a huge outdoor celebration, is one of several festivals observed by modern-day pagans (believers in an ancient religion that worships nature, which many people today are reviving). The drama of the birth and death of their gods is performed, and the festivities include chanting, drumming, and dancing.

The Ceremony of Lating

During the evening on Halloween, farmers in England used to carry a lit candle over the hills and fields during the hour before midnight. If the candle burned steadily all the while, it showed that the land was free of witchcraft and other evil powers.

October 31: Allhallows Eve (Halloween)

For the Celts, an ancient people who lived in the British Isles thousands of years ago, this was the evening before the Festival of Samhain, Lord of the Dead. Ghosts and evil spirits were believed to roam the land. The holiday on November 1

It is bad luck to eat blackberries on Halloween.

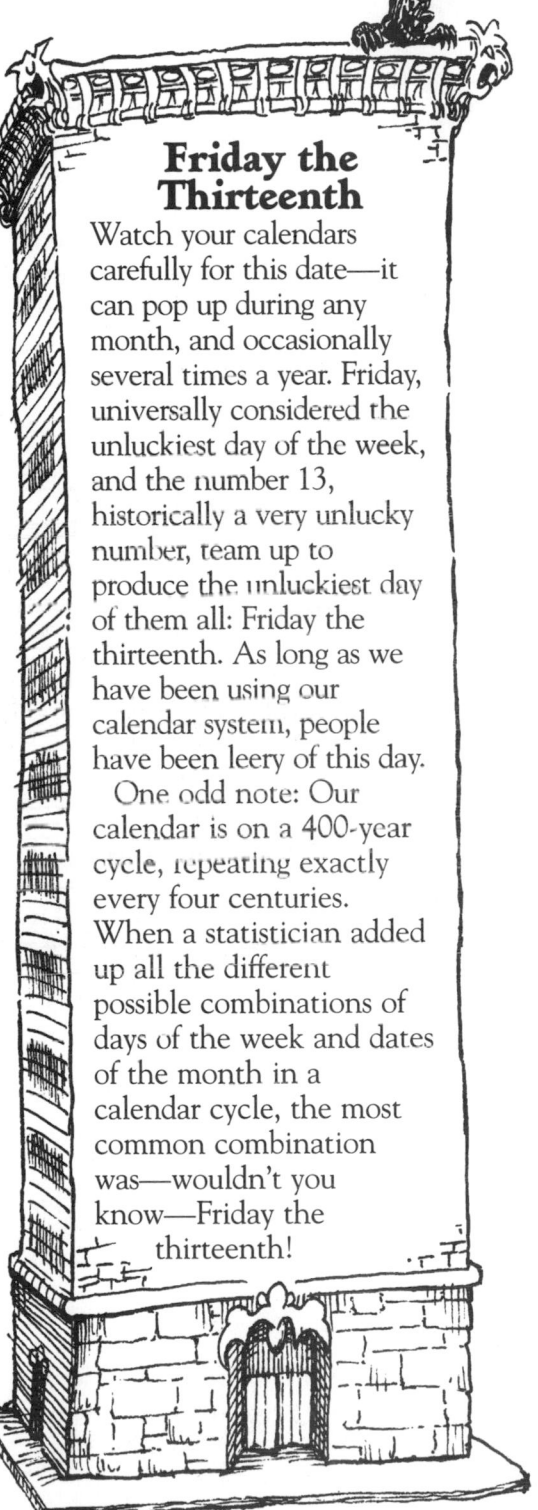

Friday the Thirteenth

Watch your calendars carefully for this date—it can pop up during any month, and occasionally several times a year. Friday, universally considered the unluckiest day of the week, and the number 13, historically a very unlucky number, team up to produce the unluckiest day of them all: Friday the thirteenth. As long as we have been using our calendar system, people have been leery of this day.

One odd note: Our calendar is on a 400-year cycle, repeating exactly every four centuries. When a statistician added up all the different possible combinations of days of the week and dates of the month in a calendar cycle, the most common combination was—wouldn't you know—Friday the thirteenth!

was later changed to a Christian celebration of the saints—All Saints' Day. But the night before—Allhallows Eve—remains a night of mystery and dread, when evil forces are free to do as they will.

November 1: Samhain (the "fire of peace")
During the harvest festival of the Druids, human sacrifice was a major part of the festivities.

November 2: All Souls' Day
English legend has it that two people stumbling around a darkened room at midnight on All Souls' Day will never see each other again.

December 28: Innocents' Day
The English believe this is a very unlucky day to get married.

FRIEND OR FOE?

Most of us go about our daily lives unable to levitate or work magic. However, there are some who are not so restricted. Either by accident of birth or through years of study, witches and magicians are able to manipulate forces, demons, and spirits to do their bidding. Read on to learn about the supernatural powers of these special, and sometimes scary, people.

WHICH IS WITCH?

Double, double, toil and trouble;
Fire burn and cauldron bubble.

—William Shakespeare, *Macbeth*

What is a witch? Our stereotypical idea of a witch is an ugly old crone stirring a cauldron, flying on a broomstick, and casting evil spells. This picture is far from true, and it arose during the Middle Ages, between the years 500 and 1500, when there was an intense, irrational fear of witchcraft. Real witches are very different.

REAL WITCHES

Nearly every culture in the world has had witches. They were special people who learned how to control the ways of nature; they knew which herbs healed and which were harmful, they could call up spirits, and they knew powerful charms and rituals. In fact, the word *witch* comes from the Anglo-Saxon word *wicca*, which means "to know." When people were in trouble or needed advice, they visited a witch. People consulted witches when they were sick, when they wanted someone to fall in love with them, or when they wanted to find something they had lost.

FEAR OF WITCHCRAFT

During the Middle Ages people became afraid of witches. Religious leaders claimed that witches were working for the Devil, doing his evil work on Earth. Demonologists, self-proclaimed experts in the practices of witches, wrote books describing the horrors of witchcraft, all of it made up: how witches ate babies, sank ships by bringing about thunderstorms, and sent spirits to murder their neighbors. In reality, witches never worshiped the Devil; they worshiped the Earth and the forces of nature. (There are some people today who call themselves "Satanists" and claim they worship the Devil. They should not be confused with witches.)

No evidence was ever presented that any witch had ever really harmed anyone. Some judges believed the accusations of greedy or jealous neighbors (many of whom later claimed the property of the convicted witch), and thousands of innocent people were burned or hanged as witches.

MYTHS ABOUT WITCHES

Go back now to the fifteenth century and discover some of the tools and rituals that demonologists of the Middle Ages claimed witches practiced or used. You'll learn that being a witch, or simply being accused of being one, meant a certain, torturous death.

PACT WITH THE DEVIL: Making a pact with the Devil, demonologists claimed, was the key to becoming a witch. It was a formal contract, written out and signed in the person's blood. Usually this agreement promised wealth and power in exchange for a person's soul.

FAMILIAR SPIRIT: According to English witchcraft experts, each witch possessed a little demon of his or her own. This demon, called a familiar, usually took the form of a small animal—a cat or a frog, for instance. The demon told the witch how to perform certain spells and also did chores for the witch—especially evil ones, up to and including murder. Sometimes the little creature was visible only to its owner.

THE WITCH'S SABBAT: During the Middle Ages, people believed that witches flew on broomsticks to sabbats, huge celebrations held in deserted fields or on forbidding mountain peaks. Once there, medieval witch-hunters claimed, the witches did such unnatural things as dance back to back; eat cakes made of salt, honey, wine, meal, oil, and blood; and drink out of horses' skulls. Many witch experts believed the Devil himself was present at these meetings, riding to the celebration on a goat with a human face. He would call the roll from a book, and the witches would respond by telling of the evil deeds they had committed since the last sabbat.

FLYING OINTMENT: People believed that, in order to fly, a witch must first be covered from head to toe with a horrible "flying ointment." The prosecutor at one witch trial produced a recipe for this ointment: the ingredients included diced-up pieces of toads, serpents, and wolves, a splash of human blood, a mixture of roots and herbs, and boiled children.

Witches actually do not need broomsticks to fly. Witches need broomsticks only for steering.

Ah, the Expense of a Good Torture!

Medieval torturers had a reputation for "padding" their expense accounts—asking to be paid more than they deserved. Finally, in 1757, the courts had had enough of their cheating. The judges drew up a list of every possible thing that could be done to a witch, along with the fees and expenses that would be paid for those services.

Following are some of the actual items on that list:

For terrorizing by showing the instruments of torture	6 shillings
For arranging and crushing the thumb	12 shillings
For burning with a hot iron	6 shillings
For cutting out the tongue, and then burning the mouth with a red-hot iron	18 shillings
For cutting off a hand or several fingers	6 shillings
For nailing to the gallows a cut-off tongue or chopped-off hand	8 shillings

WITCH TRIALS

In the fifteenth century, witchcraft trials began in earnest and continued for more than 300 years. More than 300,000 people throughout Europe, most of them innocent of any crime, were put to death as witches. The hysteria became so fierce that once someone was accused of being a witch, the person could do almost nothing to prove his or her innocence.

thumbscrews

The only way to convict someone in a witchcraft trial was to get the witch's confession. As this was usually accomplished by torture, it is not too surprising that many innocent people

spine-roller

confessed. Among the tools of the torturer's trade were the eye-gouger, branding iron, and spine-roller—a device that looked like an iron rolling pin covered with heavy spikes. The thumbscrew was another; it was a metal band that fit over the knuckle of the thumb with a screw that could be turned until the thumb was crushed. The accused witches were tortured until they confessed, and then they were burned or hanged.

eye-gougers

WITCHCRAFT TODAY

Are there witches today? You bet, but nobody knows how many. After centuries of being hunted down and killed, it is understandable that most of today's witches tend to keep their beliefs secret. However, it is known that modern witches, many of whom call themselves "wiccans," do not worship the Devil or practice black magic. Some claim that their covens go back hundreds, even thousands, of years. In fact, many call their practice "the Old Religion."

Witches today have a great reverence for nature and all forms of life. Magic is used only to help and heal; harmful magic, they believe, will only end up hurting the person who cast the spell.

The Good, the Bad, and the Witchy

These are some of the most famous witches of fact and fiction:
- Glinda the Good Witch (from *The Wizard of Oz*)
- The Wicked Witch of the West (from *The Wizard of Oz*)
- The Witch of Endor in the Bible, consulted by Saul
- The Weird Sisters (the three witches from Shakespeare's *Macbeth*)
- Hansel and Gretel's witch
- Snow White's witch (who transformed herself from an evil queen)
- Samantha Stevens of the TV series *Bewitched*
- Broomhilda (the comic strip witch)

STRANGE SORCERY

**What charms, what conjuration,
And what mighty magic.
—William Shakespeare, *Othello***

When you hear the word *magician*, you probably think of a stage entertainer who performs illusions for the enjoyment of others. But originally, hundreds of years ago, a magician was a person who spent his or her life studying and using ancient tomes filled with instructions for conjuring up spirits and commanding them to do the magician's bidding. The magician would use this power to create fortunes, gain love, or destroy enemies. Magic was, and is, *occult* (which means "hidden") and is performed by *adepts* (students of the secret lore). There are many people who still practice real magic today.

MAGIC TERMS TO KNOW

These terms may not help you cast a spell on your homework, but read them to learn a bit about the mystical and mysterious.

BLACK MAGIC: Black magic includes any magic spell, incantation, or ritual designed to harm or kill. Black magic also includes any magic that is used to selfishly increase the power of the magician.

WHITE MAGIC: White magic includes magic spells that are designed to cure or heal, drive away storms, bring happiness, or in any other way bring positive results. Good magic is supposed to help people.

CONJURATION: Conjuration is the act of raising spirits and demons to utilize their powers. To master this grim art, the magician must spend years in study to gain the skill and willpower needed to control the forces he conjures up. This type of magic is very dangerous, and unless magicians are prepared both mentally and spiritually, and have taken the necessary precautions, they could be destroyed by the very supernatural forces they unleash.

Ouija Boards: A Method of Conjuration or an Innocent Game?

The word *ouija* (pronounced "wee-je") comes from a combination of the French and German words for "yes" (*oui* and *ja*). It is a flat piece of smooth wood, with the letters of the alphabet written on it, along with the words "Yes" and "No" and the numbers 0 through 9. Participants place their fingers on a small pointer, called a planchette, and ask questions. The planchette begins to slide across the board, pointing at letters and spelling out words.

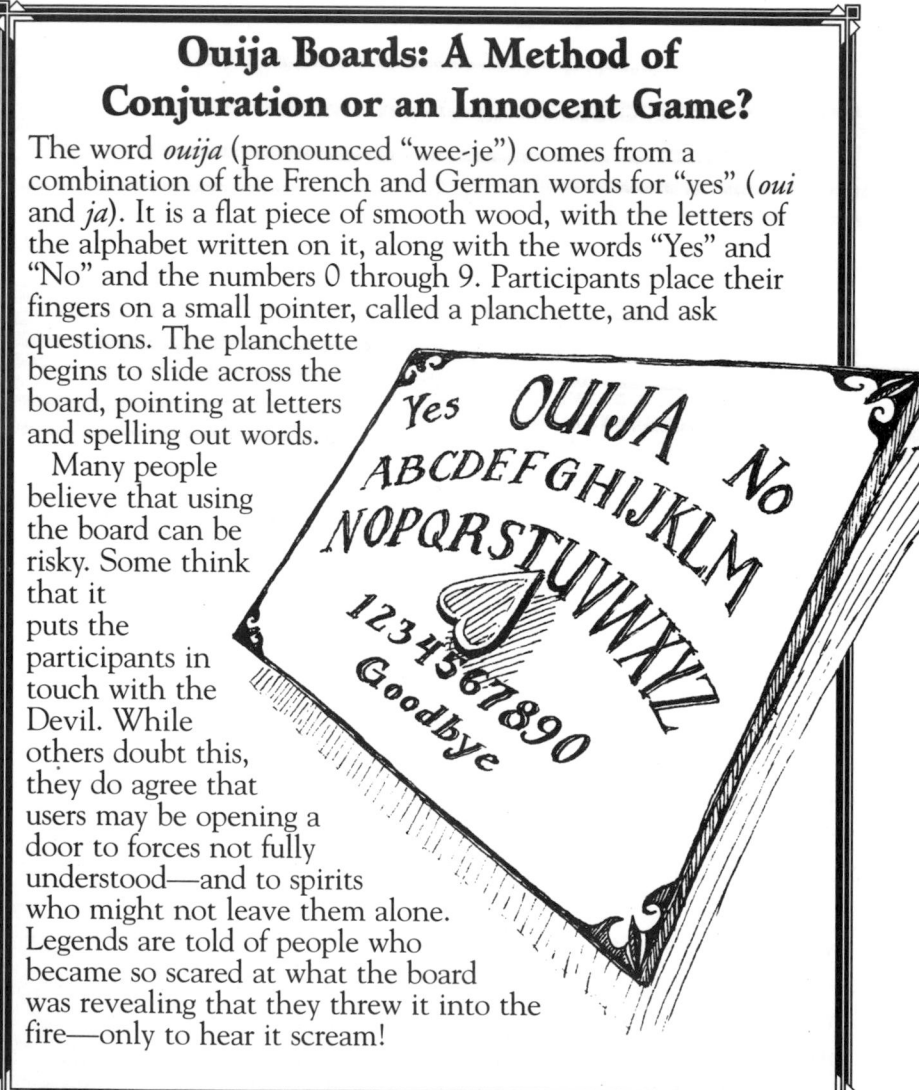

Many people believe that using the board can be risky. Some think that it puts the participants in touch with the Devil. While others doubt this, they do agree that users may be opening a door to forces not fully understood—and to spirits who might not leave them alone. Legends are told of people who became so scared at what the board was revealing that they threw it into the fire—only to hear it scream!

GRIMOIRES (PRONOUNCED "GRIM-*WÄRZ*"):

These are ancient textbooks of magic containing step-by-step instructions for conjuring up spirits and demons safely and—perhaps most importantly—for commanding them to leave when they've finished their work. Some of these books contain instructions for white magic, but many describe the rituals of black magic.

SIGIL (PRONOUNCED "SIG-L"):

A sigil is a symbol a magician uses to capture and control spirits and demons. Some sigils are so dangerous that simply drawing a demon's sigil or saying its name may conjure it up.

MAGIC CIRCLE:

A magic circle is a huge seal, perhaps six feet in diameter, that magicians draw on the floor to protect themselves from the demons they raise. Signs, sigils, and magic words are part of the design. If a magician steps outside the circle, or is careless enough to let his or her arm cross over the line drawn on the floor, it means instant death—or worse!—as the raised demon is free to do whatever it wants to the magician.

SPELLS AND OINTMENTS

(Don't try any of these spells yourself! You could be blinded, burned, kicked by a bull ... or worse!)

Spells are formulas that cause or influence events. They can be written or spoken. Ointments are preparations, like medicines, that are used in magical rites for many different purposes. For example, one ointment included in the ancient grimoires was used for seeing spirits. Its recipe called for combining the gall of a bull (a foul liquid produced by the animal's liver), ants' eggs, and the fat of a white hen, and dabbing the mixture into one's eyes. This was said to give the power to see invisible spirits. A spell to see the future called for mixing linseed, psyllium seed, violet roots, and wild parsley, throwing the mixture into a fire, and allowing the smoke to blow over the person casting the spell. The future was said to then unfold before the user's eyes.

LET'S GIVE A HAND TO THE AUTHOR OF THIS SPELL!: The ancient grimoires suggested that readers who wanted to make themselves invisible should go at night to a 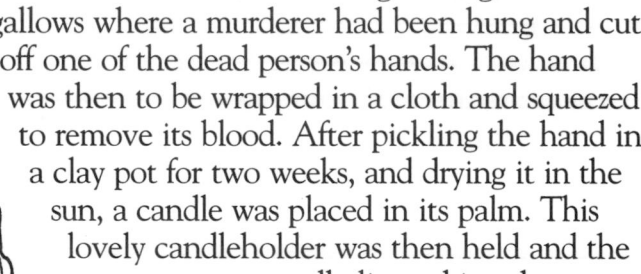 gallows where a murderer had been hung and cut off one of the dead person's hands. The hand was then to be wrapped in a cloth and squeezed to remove its blood. After pickling the hand in a clay pot for two weeks, and drying it in the sun, a candle was placed in its palm. This lovely candleholder was then held and the candle lit, making the person holding the hand invisible. (Don't try this— it will make you smell gross and be subject to criminal prosecution!)

FAMOUS MAGICIANS

You may have thought the first magician was Harry Houdini, but think again. Houdini, who died on Halloween in 1926, performed magic tricks—illusions that entertained people—as some magicians do today. But the magicians who follow performed magic for different intentions . . . sometimes scary intentions.

KING SOLOMON, TENTH CENTURY B.C.: The magicians of the Middle Ages considered King Solomon a magician and wonder worker. They believed that after studying ancient and forbidden lore, Solomon was able to conjure up spirits at will. Angered by seventy-two prideful demons, he sealed them in a brass urn and threw them into a deep lake. The men who guided his ship thought the container was filled with riches and went back to recover the urn. When they broke it open, the demons escaped. Known as the Spirits of Solomon, these demons are listed in a book called *The Lemegeton,* one of the most popular grimoires among practicing magicians today.

DR. FAUSTUS, SIXTEENTH CENTURY: A professional sorcerer in Germany, Faustus claimed he had sold his soul to the Devil in exchange for power. Although some people considered him a con man, others treated him with a great deal of respect ... and fear. When he died under mysterious circumstances, many people believed that he was killed by the Devil, who had come at last to claim his soul. Many versions of his story were written. Two of the most famous are *Dr. Faustus,* by Christopher Marlowe (1588), and *Faust,* by Goethe (in two parts, published in 1808 and 1832).

DR. LAMB, BIRTH UNKNOWN – 1640: Dr. Lamb was the personal physician of the duke of Buckingham in England. He was also known to be a sorcerer, well versed in the dark arts. Once, in front of eyewitnesses, he conjured up a tiny tree in his living room and then tiny woodsmen who chopped it down. It was incidents such as these that eventually led to his being stoned to death by a fearful and angry mob.

ALEISTER CROWLEY, 1875–1947: An English newspaper called Aleister Crowley "the wickedest man in the world." Even as a child he loved to see blood and read about torture. His strict mother called him "the beast." When he was a young man, Aleister left home to travel and learn about the world. Rumors abounded that people who crossed him suffered terrible accidents. He joined an occult group called the Hermetic Order of the Golden Dawn, but he fought with the leader. They began to attack each other mentally, sending "astral vampires" and other demons after each other. Crowley left the group and began his own Order of the Silver Star. Several years later, Crowley claimed that an invisible being named Aiwaz dictated a book to him called *The Book of the Law,* giving a new law for mankind to follow. Crowley's followers still believe in and use the book.

CURSES!

"Na!"

—An old Greek curse

(It means, simply, "There!")

The motive may be hate, revenge, or envy. The words may be whispered, shouted, or written. But all curses, at their core, have one thing in common: they have the power to hurt ... or kill. And unlike magic, curses are not hidden lore requiring years of study; curses are well known to the people of their own culture and can be cast by anyone. Following are a few ways people around the world have attempted to make, cast, and send curses.

BONE POINTING: This is a murder technique used by the aborigines of Australia. The killer takes a kangaroo bone, carves a point at one end, and drills a hole at the other. He passes a single strand of hair through the hole and ties it in place. He then points the bone at his victim, who will soon become sick and die. This may be the perfect crime, because Australian law doesn't consider it murder.

ORANGE ROT: In Italy and parts of England, an orange is used to represent the heart of a victim. The victim's name is written on a scrap of parchment and pinned to the orange. Then the fruit is placed in a chimney. As the orange rots, the victim dies a particularly gruesome death as his flesh rots away from his bones.

SENDING THE DEAD: In Haitian voodoo, evil sorcerers go to a cemetery with an offering of food and take away a handful of graveyard dirt for each person they want dead. The sorcerer spreads the dirt where he knows his victim will walk. After the victim walks on the dirt, he begins wasting away. He soon spits up blood and finally dies—unless he realizes what is happening to him and goes to a more powerful priest, who will chase the dead away.

FREAKY PHENOMENA

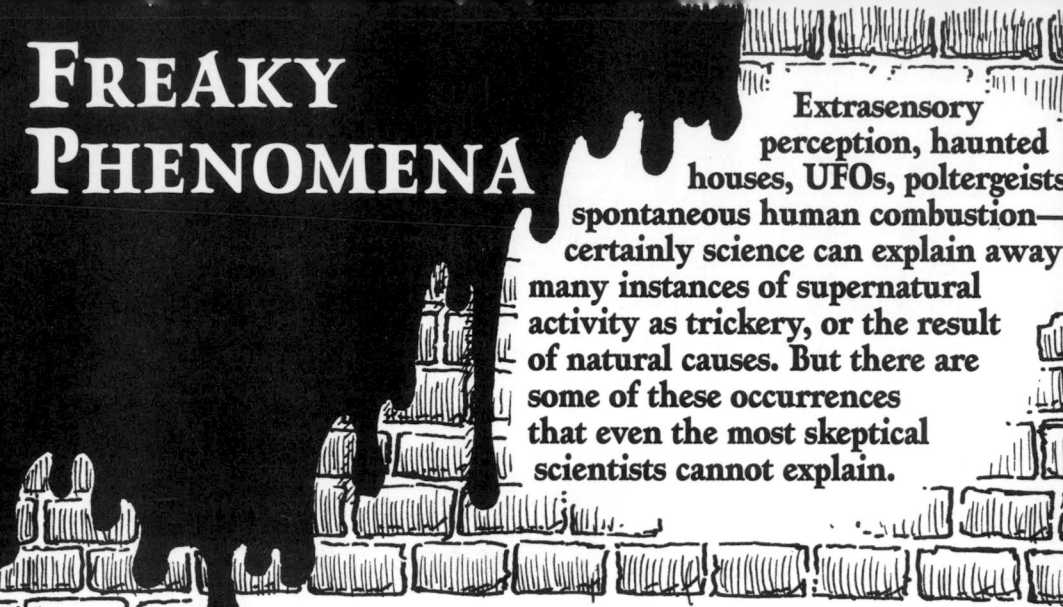

Extrasensory perception, haunted houses, UFOs, poltergeists, spontaneous human combustion—certainly science can explain away many instances of supernatural activity as trickery, or the result of natural causes. But there are some of these occurrences that even the most skeptical scientists cannot explain.

POLTERGEISTS, APPARITIONS & HAUNTS

From ghoulies and ghosties and long-leggety beasties
And things that go bump in the night,
Good Lord, deliver us!

—Anonymous Scottish prayer, c. 1800

A door opens and closes when no one is there. A stone suddenly—*impossibly*—flies past your head. A beautiful woman smiles at you, turns, and walks through a solid wall. Could you have encountered a ghost? Maybe. But what exactly *is* a ghost? The restless spirit of a dead person? Or a psychic impression of an event that happened long ago? Experts on ghosts—parapsychologists, occult researchers, mediums, even "ghostbusters"—don't agree on *exactly* what a ghost is. But they do agree that there are three different types of ghostly phenomena: poltergeists, apparitions, and haunts.

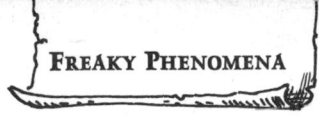

POLTERGEISTS

The word *poltergeist* comes from the German words *polter* ("a noise") and *geist* ("a spirit"). Poltergeists are noisy, invisible spirits, and they can be quite destructive. They throw small objects, move heavy furniture, and break things. Some poltergeists even communicate with the people living in the house they are affecting, usually by answering questions with knocks or raps.

In the early 1930s, researchers from Duke University in Durham, North Carolina (a major center for investigations into the paranormal from the 1930s until the mid-1960s), noted that poltergeist activity usually happened only in households in which one member was a boy or girl between the ages of twelve and nineteen. Though he or she may be in plain sight when an object is suddenly hurled from the other side of the room, the young person, called the "poltergeist agent," does not *physically* cause the disturbances. However, this youngster may be experiencing a lot of emotional stress that he or she can't let out, having problems that he or she feels unable to discuss with anyone. This leads to frustration and rage that, researchers speculate, comes out as psychokinesis (PK), which is the ability to move objects with the mind alone.

Some investigators, however, believe that poltergeists *are* actual unhappy or angry spirits of the dead, or even demons. But they also acknowledge the importance of the poltergeist agent; these researchers believe that the spirits are somehow tapping into the young person's energy in order to cause the disturbances.

37

A Few Recent Case Histories

1960: Sauchie, Scotland

A poltergeist had been moving furniture around at the home of an eleven-year-old girl, Virginia Campbell. Usually poltergeist activity stays in one place, but in this case it followed Virginia to school. Her teacher reported that Virginia's desk rose into the air with no one touching it, and the teacher's own desk turned almost completely around while she was sitting at it.

1967: Miami, Florida

The witnesses in this case included police officers and newspaper reporters. A warehouse full of glass souvenirs, including glasses, ashtrays, and plates, was "attacked" by a poltergeist, who caused thousands of dollars worth of damage. More than 200 incidents that could not be explained through any normal means occurred in the warehouse. A nineteen-year-old worker was under suspicion and was watched closely while much of the destruction was taking place. Officers found that he could not possibly have been responsible. It seemed, however, that he was the "poltergeist agent," for when the young man left, the destruction stopped.

1983: Zakopane, Poland

Many witnesses had seen glassware, pots and pans, and silverware flying around the house where a young girl, Joasia Gajewski, lived. Witnesses included neighbors, policemen, reporters, and even the city engineer, who came to the house originally to prove it was structural damage or uneven sinking of the house that was causing things to fall off shelves. The girl was studied closely for two years by scientists in Poland. In 1987, when the investigators ran out of money, the poltergeist activity was still going on, making Joasia's case the longest-lasting poltergeist on record.

APPARITIONS

An apparition is what most people think of when they imagine a ghost. An apparition appears in the same place, doing the same thing over and over. The apparition takes no notice of the living and makes no attempt to communicate.

Some researchers think an apparition is a kind of impression, or vibration, that has somehow been recorded by the place itself. Apparently a strong emotional moment has been captured on a sort of spiritual "videotape" and is being replayed.

Other paranormal researchers think that apparitions are indeed the spirits of people who died violently or unexpectedly and who may not even realize they are dead. They are trapped on earth, doomed to repeat their last actions until they are released by exorcism or other means.

HAUNTS

Haunts are phenomena that combine elements of both apparitions and poltergeists. Unlike a poltergeist, there seems to be an intelligence at work, and the movement of objects isn't random or necessarily violent. And unlike a ghost, these apparitions will take notice of you, and may even speak.

A haunt can take place anywhere, and it may include visual apparitions, strange sounds, and physical sensations.

HAVE YOU EVER BEEN VISITED BY A WRAITH?

A sudden and unexplainable appearance of a person who, at that moment, is really miles away is called a wraith, or crisis apparition, because it happens most often during a crisis—when someone dies, is near death, or is in an accident. The apparition may be of someone who is still alive. It looks solid but can disappear or fade away. The apparition might call for help, give a warning, leave a message, or simply say good-bye.

"The Most Haunted House in England"

That is what Harry Price, an English ghost hunter, called the Borley Rectory, a big house (there were twenty-three rooms) built by the Rev. Henry D. E. Bull on top of a hill in Essex in 1863. Right after it was built, it became the object of stories involving ghosts and poltergeist activity. When the last member of the Bull family died in 1927, no one wanted to live there because of the stories of hauntings. Finally a newspaper sent a reporter to investigate, and the reporter came back claiming he had heard footsteps in empty rooms and had seen flying candelabras.

Then Harry Price became involved. He visited the rectory in 1929, and spent the next twenty years investigating and writing about the place. He spent a year living there himself, and worked with many other investigators. Among the things people saw in the rectory were the ghost of a nun, flying candlesticks, and "ghost writing" that appeared on the walls. Seen outside the rectory were the ghost of a woman on the front lawn, a headless man in the garden, and a coach pulled by two horses and driven by a headless coachman. Because these activities continued for decades, it is hard to believe that someone was playing a trick on the investigators. And because so many people saw these things, it's hard to claim that an individual was lying or mistaken. Altogether, Harry Price documented nearly 2,000 unexplainable occurrences.

INTERVIEW WITH A GHOSTBUSTER

"And this voice said 'Zool,' and then I slammed the refrigerator door and I left. . . ."
"Generally you don't see that kind of behavior in a major appliance."
—Sigourney Weaver and Bill Murray, in *Ghostbusters*

The Office of Scientific Investigation and Research (OSIR) is a private agency, based in Central California, that investigates paranormal occurrences all around the world. Since 1985 OSIR has investigated hundreds of reports of poltergeists, apparitions, haunts, cases of demonic possession, UFO abductions, and the simply unexplainable. The OSIR staff includes electrical engineers, geologists, biologists, and scientists from other disciplines. Christopher Chacon, the director of OSIR and a field investigator, is also a professional illusionist and magician, a useful talent when it comes to detecting fraud or trickery. In December 1992, he agreed to answer some questions over the telephone about his job as a real ghostbuster.

How many hauntings have you personally investigated?
Chacon: I've been involved in more than 600 investigations.

How does OSIR get involved in a case? Do people call you to tell you they've seen a ghost?
Basically, yes. People call us when something unusual has happened to them. If it's something that only happened once, they want to know if the thing can be explained rationally, or if there's a paranormal explanation. They also want to be reassured that they're not going crazy.

What do you tell them?
We tell them that what has happened could be a normal part

of our world, even though it's a part of our world that we don't fully understand.

What do you do then?
If the event is recurring [happening again and again], we will tell the people how to interact with the phenomenon or how to try to terminate it. And if they want, we will send a team out to investigate.

What do you do when you get there?
We approach every job with an open mind, without being believers or skeptics—we don't want to influence the environment with our attitude. So the first thing we do is interview the occupants and evaluate them psychologically and physically. Next we test the environment. We check for structural elements, chemicals in the environment that may be causing hallucinations, magnetic fields, houses that are tilting, anything out of the ordinary.

And if you don't find a normal explanation?
Then we begin investigating for paranormal explanations. We monitor radiation levels, gravitational fields, and temperature and lighting conditions to see if the phenomenon is leaving any kinds of physical traces. If it's not happening physically, then it's happening on a perceptual level only [affecting people's senses: sight, hearing, etc.]. About sixty to seventy percent of legitimate hauntings are perceptual.

How do you get rid of a ghost or poltergeist that is bothering people?
Generally, changing the people's frame of mind will solve the problem. We explain to them that if they are frightened of it, it will only make it worse. Often we just tell them to ignore it, if they can, until it goes away. But if it seems to be dangerous, or is affecting the environment in a way that can't be ignored—opening and slamming doors, throwing things—we can try many experimental methods, including trying to alter the environment.

What's the strangest case you have ever investigated?
Well... [long pause]. There was one case where a little boy on the East Coast woke up one night feeling strange, and then realized he could see right through his body—he was semitransparent. He jumped out of bed and ran out of his room through the door—I mean, his door was *closed* and he had run *through*

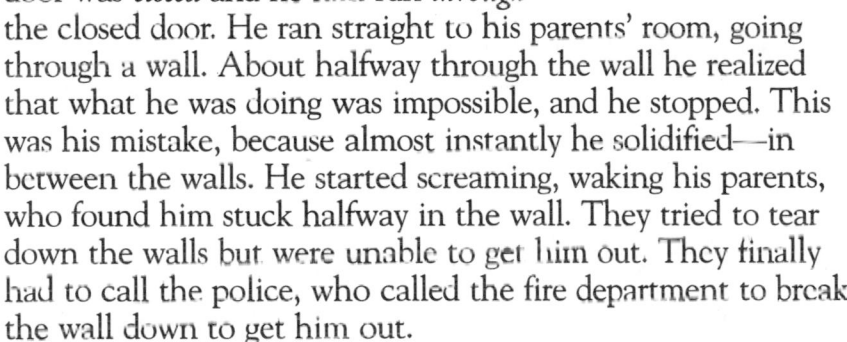

the closed door. He ran straight to his parents' room, going through a wall. About halfway through the wall he realized that what he was doing was impossible, and he stopped. This was his mistake, because almost instantly he solidified—in between the walls. He started screaming, waking his parents, who found him stuck halfway in the wall. They tried to tear down the walls but were unable to get him out. They finally had to call the police, who called the fire department to break the wall down to get him out.

That's incredible. How did you explain it?
Well, we have some theories. One is that, somehow, perhaps through psychokinesis, the boy had altered his body on the molecular level, allowing it to pass through solid matter.

What advice can you give to an aspiring ghostbuster?
The two most important things you can bring with you on a haunted house investigation are, number one, a scientific attitude—approach this as a scientific detective. Don't be skeptical, but be analytical. Try to find a normal explanation for what is occurring before you jump to a paranormal conclusion. If you go expecting to see something supernatural, you will probably convince yourself that you did. And number two, bring along a sense of humor. Many people take this stuff far too seriously, and let their fear get in the way of their investigation.

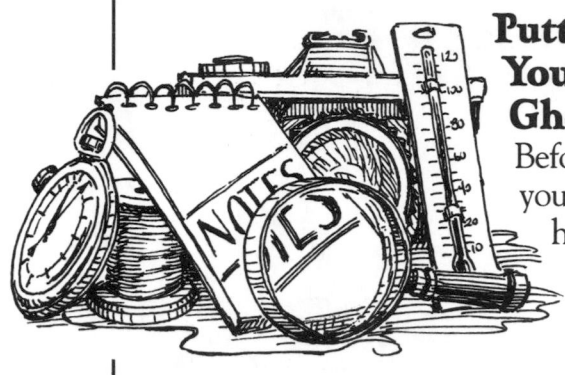

Putting Together Your Own Ghost Hunter's Kit

Before going "into the field," you should put together a ghost hunter's kit. If you should find a ghost, the following items would be handy to have around.

- ❦ **Notebook:** To jot down observations and feelings. Try to make an entry every fifteen minutes, whether anything paranormal is happening or not.
- ❦ **Tape measure:** To make accurate measurements of distances.
- ❦ **Weather thermometer:** To measure changing temperature (paranormal events are sometimes accompanied by temperature changes).
- ❦ **Camera:** Use a camera that can shoot "fast" film, with a speed of 400 or 1,000 ASA, so you can take pictures without a flash.
- ❦ **Magnifying glass:** To study small objects or ghostly smudges that may appear.
- ❦ **Small containers:** To collect any samples an apparition may leave behind.
- ❦ **Stopwatch (or a watch with a second hand):** To time the duration of manifestations.
- ❦ **Portable tape recorder:** To record any sounds the apparition makes.
- ❦ **Baby powder:** Sprinkle powder on the floor. Most real apparitions don't leave footprints. If footprints appear, someone is probably trying to trick you.
- ❦ **Masking tape:** Seal tape around windows and doors. Apparitions can pass through closed doors. If the tape is undisturbed, it's a sign you may be dealing with a genuine paranormal event.
- ❦ **Spool of thread:** Attach threads across hallways, stairs, and doorways. Apparitions should be able to pass through the threads without disturbing them.

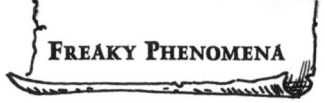

WHO YA GONNA CALL?

The following groups and institutions are interested in different kinds of paranormal phenomena. Some will try to help you if you are troubled by the things described in these pages; others will investigate; others will simply add your story to the thousands of other personal experiences they have collected.

American Society for Psychical Research
5 West 73rd Street
New York, New York 10023
This organization was founded in 1885 to study things science can't explain—haunts, ESP, and especially the survival of the spirit after death. It investigates unexplainable incidents and publishes a journal of the results of its findings.

Foundation for Research on the Nature of Man
Institute for Parapsychology
P.O. Box 6847, College Station
Durham, North Carolina 27708
This organization researches puzzling or unexplainable experiences that offer glimpses into the untapped potential of human beings. If you see a crisis apparition, encounter a UFO, have a psychic experience, or witness some other unexplainable occurrence, write to this group about it.

OSIR (Office of Scientific Investigation and Research)
P.O. Box 461779
Los Angeles, California 90046
OSIR investigates all kinds of unexplained phenomena, from ghosts and hauntings to UFO encounters, demonic possession, and the unexplainable. The organization offers counseling and, if necessary, will send a team to your home to investigate.

Parapsychological Association
P.O. Box 3695
Charlottesville, North Carolina 22903-3695
This organization was founded by the father of ESP testing, Dr. J. B. Rhine. Its goal is to offer a scientific approach to parapsychology and to get information out to other scientists. The group often needs volunteers for ESP experiments.

IT'S A BIRD ...
IT'S A PLANE ... IT'S AN ALIEN!

... This world was being watched keenly and closely by intelligences greater than man's ... intellects vast and cool and unsympathetic, regarded this earth with envious eyes, and slowly and surely drew their plans against us.

—H. G. Wells, *The War of the Worlds*

On June 24, 1947, a pilot searching for an airplane that had crashed in the Cascade Mountains in Washington State looked up and saw nine bright disk-shaped objects in the sky. They flew past him in two lines at a speed he estimated to be 1,600 miles per hour. The pilot, Kenneth Arnold, said they looked like "saucers skipped over water," and the phrase "flying saucers" was born.

That same year, three unidentified flying objects (UFOs) were sighted over Roswell, New Mexico. Shocked observers saw them crash. The U.S. Air Force said they were only weather balloons, but many people still claim that the government is storing the bodies of three aliens in a freezer in a warehouse in the New Mexico desert.

A fear of flying saucers spread across the United States. Newspapers reported numerous sightings. People were terrified that the Earth would be invaded by aliens from outer space. Scientists scoffed, and no physical evidence was produced, and eventually the hubbub quieted down ... but sightings and other unexplainable happenings continue. Read about a few of the strangest occurrences.

UFOs OVER THE WHITE HOUSE: On July 20, 1952, radar screens at three different air bases began tracking seven UFOs in the airspace over the White House. People could see them from the ground. A fighter aircraft was launched to see close up what these things were. As the pilot neared one, all three took off at speeds greater than that of any earthly aircraft—and the images faded off the radar screens.

FIRST CONTACT WITH AN ALIEN: One of the first reported cases of a human being encountering aliens outside of a spacecraft occurred on July 1, 1965. A farmer in France saw an oval craft in his field. He snuck up close and saw two creatures the size of boys, with large skulls, and eyes that were slanted and longer than human eyes. Their mouths were mere slits in their faces, and their chins came to a point. The creatures pointed some kind of stick at the farmer, and he fell to the ground, unable to move. The beings got into their ship and flew away. After that, the plants where the ship had landed died, and none have grown there ever since.

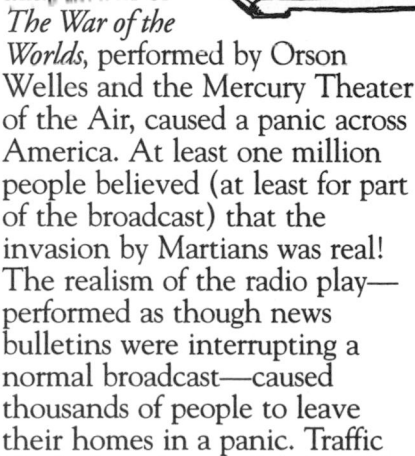

The Great Invasion

On the evening of October 30, 1938, a radio adaptation of *The War of the Worlds,* performed by Orson Welles and the Mercury Theater of the Air, caused a panic across America. At least one million people believed (at least for part of the broadcast) that the invasion by Martians was real! The realism of the radio play—performed as though news bulletins were interrupting a normal broadcast—caused thousands of people to leave their homes in a panic. Traffic blocked roads out of major cities as people took to the streets.

UFO ABDUCTIONS: Hundreds of people claim that aliens have taken them against their will aboard flying saucers. Some of these people believe that they have been watched by aliens since they were children. They remember incidents of "missing time" when they were kids—playing outside or walking home, and suddenly finding themselves in a different place along the same road or in another part of the woods. They would later notice scars on their bodies that they had never seen before. And they would have nightmares or wisps of memories about strange laboratories and creatures with large eyes. These people are convinced that they were implanted with some kind of monitoring device, or tagged the way scientists tag animals to monitor their movements. Many abductees believe they are part of some type of alien scientific investigation, and that they are occasionally recaptured for further experiments, only to have their memories wiped clean.

Can You Identify These UFO Movies?

The Day the Earth Stood Still (1951)
Invaders from Mars (1953)
It Came from Outer Space (1953)
War of the Worlds (1953)
Earth vs. the Flying Saucers (1956)
Close Encounters of the Third Kind (1977)
E.T. the Extra-Terrestrial (1982)
Fire in the Sky (1993)

Other people who claim they were kidnapped by aliens feel it happened randomly; they simply stumbled across a UFO in a clearing or were followed by one as they were driving down a road. Later, under hypnosis, they remember many details of physical exams and of probes being inserted into their bodies.

After a UFO encounter many people, whether abducted or not, show signs of stress, anxiety, and night terrors. But one of the most unusual—and scary—aftereffects of a UFO encounter is a visit from the Men in Black.

MEN IN BLACK: In many cases, after someone encounters a UFO, three men dressed in black suits come to the person's home or office and issue a warning to stop telling stories about the experience. They threaten and badger and try to convince people that they didn't see what they thought they did. One person who was researching UFOs was told by a Man in Black, "If you don't stop, we'll kill you." At least one death has been connected to Men in Black.

Who are the Men in Black? Are they government agents? Or are they aliens trying to keep their presence a secret? Some people believe that they are simply the fantasies of the individuals who report them, but these strange men have also been seen by several impartial witnesses.

Be on the Lookout!

Have you seen these men? The Men in Black arrive in a new black car, usually a Cadillac. They have dark complexions, their hair is growing strangely, and their voices come out in a strange, flat monotone or a scratchy whine. They claim to be working for the Air Force or other government agency, and they flash an official-looking I.D. card. But they usually visit the person *before* he or she has had a chance to contact the police, Air Force, or any other officials.

WHAT ARE FORTEAN PHENOMENA?

**There are more things in heaven and earth ...
than are dreamt of in your philosophy.**
—William Shakespeare, *Hamlet*

Charles Fort, born in New York in 1874, made it his life's work to collect reports of odd and unexplainable occurrences. Fort sought out and compiled newspaper stories, firsthand accounts, and other records of these and many more events that science could not, or would not, explain. In 1931, the year before Fort died, the Fortean Society was founded to study and publicize unusual events such as those listed below.

- Amazing coincidences.
- Bleeding statues and paintings of religious icons in churches or homes that, for no explainable reason, begin to ooze red fluid. In some cases the fluid has been analyzed and proven to be blood!
- Blobs and growths on city sidewalks and streets.
- Encounters with mysterious creatures, such as Mothman, a tall, gray, manlike being with a ten-foot wingspan who has been spotted several times in the Ohio River Valley.
- Rains of blood, stones, living fish, frogs, and other objects, which fall from the sky.

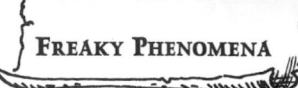

- Levitation experiences, where people have the ability to float in the air.

- Family jinxes, where families or individuals have incredible strings of bad luck—or bring bad luck to others!

- Spontaneous human combustion, where a person suddenly, and for no apparent reason, catches on fire—a fire that starts inside the body, then breaks out on the skin!

> **TERRIFYING TIDBIT**:
> One expert studying the remains of an apparently spontaneously combusted body in 1960 found that the heat had been so intense, it should have burned down the entire apartment building! Yet the fire stayed in a tight circle around the person as she sat in a chair, watching TV.

- Twins who suffer identical injuries although miles apart.

- Unexplainable appearances and disappearances, where people vanish without a trace, or suddenly appear miles— or *years*—from where they are supposed to be.

- Unexplained lights, such as the Joplin Lights that appear to bounce and move with intelligence on an empty field in Joplin, Missouri. No one can get close enough to them to examine them; they keep hopping away, and there is no explanation for them.

Spontaneous Human Combustion (SHC)

One of the scariest of all Fortean phenomena is spontaneous human combustion. Once a person begins burning, it is only seconds before the body is entirely consumed by flames and the fire burns itself out. The body is reduced to ashes— and yet nothing else in the room, *sometimes not even the person's clothing*, is touched by the flames. There have been dozens of cases reported over the years. How does the fire start? How does it go out? No one knows how—or who will be struck next.

51

FRIGHTENING FACTS

What a scary place this world can be. And what scary things there are in it. Places to go, people to see—or to avoid! Dangerous animals, real and ... maybe real. Come now on a whirlwind tour of the scariest people, places, animals, and *things* on earth.

PECULIAR PLACES

I traveled among unknown men,
In lands beyond the sea.
—William Wordsworth, "I Traveled Among Unknown Men"

What makes some places scarier than others? What forces, natural or supernatural, combine to give a patch of land, or a body of water, or an entire country an aura of foreboding and terror? Is there really something there—something unseen, yet somehow sensed? Read on, and decide for yourself....

STONEHENGE

A circle of huge stone slabs on Salisbury Plain in Wiltshire, England, Stonehenge dates from before written history. *Stonehenge* means "hanging stones." No one knows who put them there, or why. Some say Merlin, King Arthur's magician, built Stonehenge during the Middle Ages. Others say it may have been used as a landing site for UFOs. Many people claim that the stones possess magical powers, and many report seeing strange lights and unexplainable sounds around the stones. Modern-day witches and pagans come to Stonehenge for their major festivals.

THE BERMUDA TRIANGLE

Also known as the Devil's Triangle, the Bermuda Triangle fills an area of the Atlantic Ocean whose three corners are marked by Florida, Bermuda, and Puerto Rico. More than one hundred airplanes and ships have mysteriously disappeared without a trace inside the Bermuda Triangle. One moment an airplane is there, the next it is simply gone; radar blips have just disappeared off the middle of the screen.

The first modern report of a disappearance in this area was on December 5, 1945, when six Navy planes disappeared without a trace. One of the final contacts between the flight leader and the control tower reveals the strange circumstances surrounding the disappearance:

> *Flight leader:* Calling Tower. This is an emergency...
> *Tower:* What is your position?
> *Flight leader:* We are not sure of our position .... we seem to be lost....
> *everything is wrong*... even the ocean doesn't look as it should.

What could the pilot have meant by this last cryptic comment? We will never know for sure because contact was soon lost, and the planes and flight personnel were never seen again.

Of course, thousands of ships and planes pass safely through the Bermuda Triangle every year. But many people who pass through have reported seeing balls of fire and explosions in the sky. Airplane crews have reported that their compasses begin spinning wildly, or that they have felt as if they were being pulled down toward the sea. What is the cause? Are there UFOs hidden under the ocean? Are aliens kidnapping people for some unknown purpose? Or is there a rational explanation for each and every disappearance? To this day, nobody knows the answer.

Christopher Columbus Meets the Bermuda Triangle

The first written report indicating the mysterious nature of the area came from Christopher Columbus on one of his voyages of discovery. While he was in the area of the Bermuda Triangle, Columbus wrote in his log that his compass began acting strangely, and he noted that an unearthly light seemed to be coming from *under the water*.

CROP CIRCLES

Throughout southern England, large circles and other patterns appear overnight in the middle of fields of crops. Some unknown force flattens but doesn't crush the crops, forming the patterns in the fields.

The circles may be as large as 300 feet across, or as small as ten feet. Lately crop circles have begun appearing in more and more elaborate patterns: lines and squiggles, mazes with ornate borders, spiral designs. Since the 1980s hundreds of crop circles have been found, and the phenomenon has spread to America.

Farmers on whose lands the crop circles appear say they have seen lights at night hovering over the fields. This has led some to guess that crop circles are messages from UFOs— messages that have yet to be decoded. Scientists have theorized that some unknown force of nature is responsible, but so far no answer to the mystery has been found.

HORRIBLE HUMANS

**O villain, villain, smiling, damned villain! ...
That one may smile, and smile, and be a villain.**
—William Shakespeare, *Hamlet*

Murderers. Real-life monsters. Bloodthirsty men and women. Come say hello to some of the scariest people in history you'd *never* want to meet.

VLAD TEPES
(VLAD THE IMPALER) (1431–1476)

Vlad Tepes, the ruler of Transylvania, was also called Dracula, which means both "the Devil" and "dragon." The title character of the novel *Dracula,* about the greatest vampire of all time, was based on this monstrous ruler.

Known far and wide for his cruelty, Vlad skinned people, cut them into pieces, or buried them alive. But his favorite method of killing was impalement: Starting from the bottom of the torso, his henchmen slowly pushed a sharpened  wooden pole upward through the victim's body. They did it slowly, with great care, so the victim wouldn't die right away. Then the pole was fixed upright in the ground where the victim would die, writhing in pain. Vlad impaled hundreds of people at a time, then enjoyed dining outdoors, among them. When one of his officers complained about the stench, Vlad immediately had the man impaled—but on a higher stake, so he would not have to smell the others.

Vlad died in a battle with the Turks. His head was cut off and sent to the Turkish sultan at Constantinople, where it was exhibited on a tall wooden pole.

> **TERRIFYING TIDBIT:**
> A group of Turkish ambassadors did not remove their turbans in the presence of Vlad the Impaler. They explained that it was their custom to keep their heads covered. Vlad reportedly said, "Very well, let me help you keep your custom," and ordered their turbans nailed to their heads.

COUNTESS ELIZABETH BÁTHORY, 1560–1614

Afraid of growing old, Countess Bathory of Hungary became convinced that if she bathed in the blood of young girls, she could stay young forever. For ten years she drained the blood of imprisoned girls so that she could take "blood baths" in a huge iron vat. After one intended victim escaped, the king of Hungary ordered his soldiers to storm her castle. They found the bodies of several girls who had been drained of their blood, along with others who were barely alive but whose bodies had been punctured. Soldiers bricked up the countess inside her room, with only a small opening through which she was given food. There she remained for the rest of her days.

JACK THE RIPPER, NINETEENTH CENTURY

Jack the Ripper was the name given to the murderer of seven women in London in 1888. He slit their throats and mutilated their bodies. The crimes were never solved officially, and the identity of the Ripper remains a mystery.

According to one of several theories, however, the mystery was solved and then covered up. According to this story, a psychic had a vision of a murder that was about to happen, so he went to the police. The police didn't listen to him, and a killing took place just as he had described it. The police paid more attention when the psychic returned with another vision. He told the police that this time the victim would have her ears cut off. And, in fact, Jack the Ripper had sent Scotland Yard a letter saying that he was going to cut off the ears of his next victim. The psychic named a famous London doctor as Jack the Ripper. The police investigated, found that the doctor was insane, and locked him away in an asylum. Because the doctor was the queen's own physician, the royal family didn't allow his name to be released. It was announced that the doctor had suddenly died, and a mock funeral service was held for him!

LIZZIE BORDEN, 1860–1927

On August 4, 1892, Lizzie Borden's father and stepmother were murdered by an ax-wielding killer. Lizzie was arrested and put on trial. She was found *not* guilty, but many people continue to believe she committed the crimes, because of the compelling evidence against her and because she made conflicting statements under oath. Books are still written about her to this day—two in 1992 alone: one trying to prove her guilt, the other attempting to show her innocence. A rhyme was even written about her, which, by the way, is not all true. Her father was whacked only eleven times, and her stepmother twenty-one times!

Lizzie inspired the rhyme:

Lizzie Borden took an ax,
And gave her father forty whacks.
When she saw what she had done,
She gave her mother forty-one.

ED GEIN, 1906–1984

Ed Gein was a mild-mannered man who lived on a farmhouse outside Plainfield, Wisconsin. When the police came to his house to investigate a murder, however, they discovered inside masks made of the faces of ten human heads; belts, lampshades, and seat cushions he had made from human skin; a woman's head in a paper bag; and a box of noses. At first Gein claimed that he simply dug up fresh bodies from the local graveyard, but later he admitted to at least two murders. His story was the inspiration for *Psycho,* the novel by Robert Bloch and the classic horror film by Alfred Hitchcock.

CANNIBALS

Cannibalism, the eating of human flesh, is a practice as old as man. Below are some of the peoples who have engaged in cannibalism. It is recommended that you go on a juice fast before visiting these places, lest the locals find you plump and appetizing.

PEOPLE	PLACE
BATAK: Ate their enemies (considered all strangers enemies); sold human flesh in marketplace.	Sumatra
BIMIN-KUSKUSMIN: Ate captive enemies.	West Sepik Province, Papua New Guinea
DOBU: Ate captive enemies.	Massim, Papua New Guinea
FIJIANS: Ate captive enemies.	Fiji Islands, South Pacific
GIMI: Ate their dead as part of religious rite.	Eastern Highland Province, Papua New Guinea
HUA: Ate their dead as part of religious rite.	Eastern Highland Province, Papua New Guinea
MAORIS: Ate captive enemies.	New Zealand
MELANESIANS: Considered humans a food source; called human body "long pig."	Melanesia, South Pacific
TUPINAMBA INDIANS: Ate captive enemies.	Eastern Brazil

CREEPY CAREERS

It's a dirty job, but someone's got to do it!

—Anonymous

The mad scientist. A sorcerer's apprentice. These scary jobs may not exist—but who needs 'em? If it's a creepy career you want, get your résumés ready and check out the following mini-dictionary of occupations some folks are *dying* to break into.

Cemetery night watchman: Spends night patrolling graveyard, watching for vandals and grave robbers.

Embalmer: Embalms bodies in preparation for burial. Packs body openings with cotton soaked with embalming fluid to prevent escape of gases. Drains blood from circulatory system and replaces blood with embalming fluid. Inserts plastic strips or cotton between eyeball and eyelid to prevent slipping and sinking of eyelid. May join lips using needle and thread or wire.

Ghost hunter: Tracks down and tries to explain ghostly phenomena.

Grave digger: Digs and prepares graves in cemeteries.

The Educated Mortician

There are many colleges of mortuary science in the United States, where approximately 35,000 students are learning how to put together a funeral. The programs are very focused and strictly academic. There are no official extracurricular activities or sports programs—so don't expect to join a football team if you plan to attend Mortuary U!

Hearse driver: Drives hearse bearing coffins to their final resting place.

Morgue attendant: Prepares human body for postmortem examination.

Mortician: Directs funerals, interviews family, coordinates the transfer of the body for burial preparation, and arranges transportation to and from the cemetery.

Mortuary beautician: Performs grooming tasks on embalmed bodies (manicures nails, sets hair, etc.).

Spirit photographer: Attempts to take pictures of ghosts (a popular occupation in the 1800s).

BIZARRE BEASTS

We conjecture it is either some unknown animal, or the god that he worships.

—Jonathan Swift, *Gulliver's Travels*

The Loch Ness Monster ... the Abominable Snowman ...Mokéle-Mbêmbe. Do these creatures exist? Or are they only stories believed by superstitious natives and gullible tourists? Many scientists take stories of these and other creatures very seriously. These scientists are called cryptozoologists, and they try to find and study animals that have remained "hidden" to most of the world. Here are the facts *and* the rumors. Decide for yourself if these creatures live only in our imaginations.

Who: THE ABOMINABLE SNOWMAN, OR YETI
What: An apelike creature that walks on two feet, with dark shaggy hair covering its whole body except for the face.
Where: The Himalayan mountain range in India, Nepal, and Tibet.
First recorded sightings: In 1889, British Army Major L. A. Waddell reported finding large, bare footprints in the snow of the Himalayas in northeastern India. In 1921, Lieutenant Colonel Charles Kenneth Howard-Bury, the leader of an expedition climbing Mount Everest, actually saw creatures moving in the snow high above the climbers' position. When the members of the expedition reached the spot, the creatures were gone; but the climbers found bare

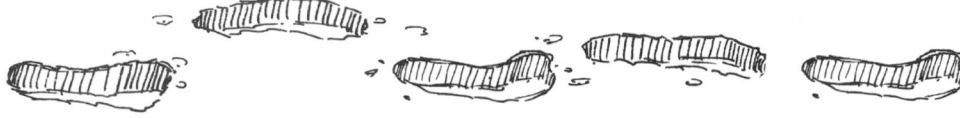

footprints. The native guides explained that the footprints were made by a *metoh-kangmi,* which means "wild man of the snow," but this was mistranslated to the world as "abominable snowman." The Sherpas, the people who live in the Himalayas, call this creature Yeti.

Habits: The Abominable Snowman, or Yeti, doesn't spend all of its time in the snow. It is believed to live at the treeline, the zone just below where the snow remains on the mountains all year long. Occasionally it travels up into the snow, but more often it seems to cautiously travel down the mountains, possibly to hunt wild yak or raid farms or villages for food.

Verdict of science: In 1951, Eric Shipton, a renowned mountain climber, took the first photographs of what many people believe to be a huge Yeti footprint. Critics claimed that melting snow distorted the footprint of another animal, possibly the Himalayan black bear, which is commonly found in the area. Until some definitive proof is found, the question of the existence of a "wild man of the snow" remains an open one. That hasn't, however, stopped the nation of Bhutan, a country in the Himalayas, from proclaiming the Yeti their national animal!

Sherpa parents warn their children that if they are being chased by a Yeti they should run downhill, because the Yeti's hair will fall over its face and cover its eyes.

Many cultures throughout Asia have legends of creatures remarkably similar to the Yeti that date back thousands of years.

Where	Creature
Ancient Babylon	Enkidu
Ancient China	Feifei
People's Republic of China	Wildman
India	Rakshasa
Nepal	Rakshi-Bompo
Mongolia	Alma

Who: BIGFOOT

What: Somewhat similar to the Yeti in appearance, Bigfoot has been described as being nearly seven feet tall and covered with hair.

Where: In the forests of the Pacific Northwest of the United States (sightings of similar creatures have been reported all around the country; see "America's Land Monsters," following).

First recorded sighting: In 1811, David Thompson, a Canadian fur trader, reported that he had seen footprints in the snow that were fourteen inches long. The Indians of the area had long told stories of giant manlike creatures. The Salish of British Columbia called them Sasquatch; the Huppas of northern California called them Ohmah, which means "wild men of the woods."

Verdict of science: In 1967, the first film was taken of a supposed Bigfoot by a former rodeo rider named Roger Patterson. Lasting only about

Close Encounters with a Real Big Shoe Size

In 1958, a bulldozer operator in northern California named Jerry Crew discovered huge footprints near a site where he was working. He made a plaster cast of one footprint. It was enormous— it reached from his shoulder to his waist. When a photo of him holding the giant footprint hit the newspapers, the name "Bigfoot" was born.

twenty seconds, the footage has been subject to endless debate. Even members of the special effects department of the Walt Disney studios analyzed the film—and they couldn't detect any fakery. Still, despite the evidence of footprints and film, most scientists reject the existence of Bigfoot. A poll in the late 1970s showed that 88 percent of them refused to even consider the possibility.

AMERICA'S LAND MONSTERS

Similar creatures have been sighted in different parts of the United States. Depending on where you live, maybe you can catch a glimpse of:

Where	Creature
Missouri	Mo-Mo
Arkansas	The Fouke Monster
Florida	The Skunk Ape
Texas	The Lake Worth Monster

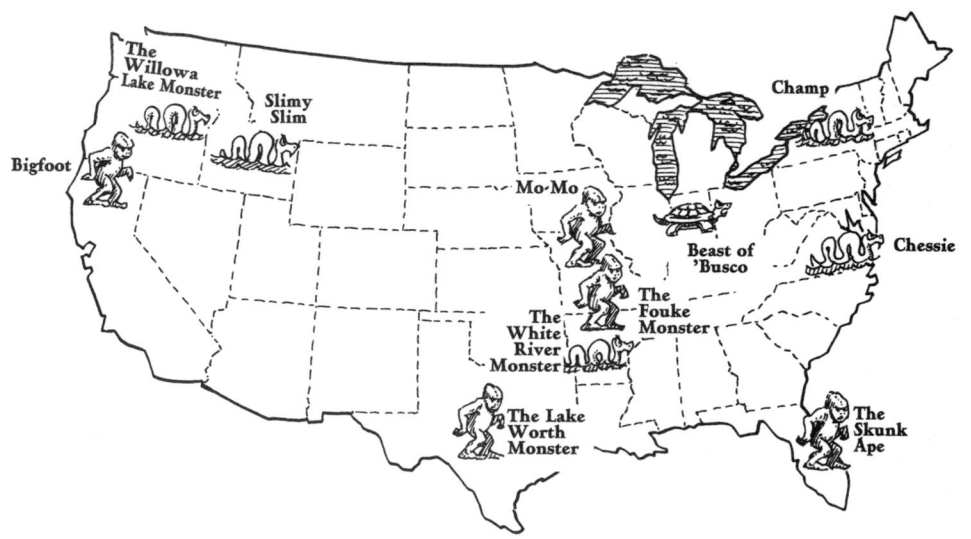

AMERICA'S WATER MONSTERS

So you want to catch a glimpse of Nessie, but you can't afford to go to Scotland? You're in luck; the United States has more than its share of purported lake and river monsters.

Where	Creature
White River, near Newport, Arkansas	White River Monster (snakelike creature the size of a railroad car)
Lake Payette, Idaho	Slimy Slim (50-foot-long reptilian creature)
Churubusco, Indiana	Beast of 'Busco (giant snapping turtle)
Lake Champlain, at the northern border of New York State	Champ (20-foot-long water snake with a horselike head)
Willowa Lake, Oregon	Willowa Lake Monster (huge, black snakelike creature)
Chesapeake Bay, Virginia, near mouth of the Potomac River	Chessie (gray, snakelike thing about 25 feet long)

Who: THE LOCH NESS MONSTER, OR NESSIE

What: A long, reptilian creature with a snakelike head. The skin appears to be dark gray and smooth. Some suspect that the creature is a plesiosaur, which most scientists believe became extinct 70 million years ago.

Where: Loch Ness, a lake in the highlands of Scotland.

First recorded sighting: In A.D. 565, Saint Columba saw a huge snakelike thing in Loch Ness and shouted to it, "Go back!" The creature, oddly enough, obeyed.

Modern sightings: On July 22, 1930, three young fishermen saw a creature at least twenty feet long, with its head three feet out of the water, come rushing toward them, causing their boat to rock. Then, in 1933, shortly after the construction of a new road around the lake, a man driving on the road claimed he saw a thirty-foot-long creature. He watched it frolic for about a minute before it plunged under the surface.

Verdict of science: In 1960, the first film was taken of the monster, and it showed a dark shape swimming rapidly. Critics scoffed, saying the object could have been a boat or a log. Then England's Royal Air Force analyzed the film. The RAF said that, without question, the object in the film was alive and could have been up to ninety feet long! In 1970, the American Academy of Applied Science brought in underwater cameras that would take a picture automatically if an object came within range. It wasn't long before they got results. One 1972 photo clearly showed a pair of large flippers. Another may have shown a face, but the image was too fuzzy to be certain.

Is there really a monster in Loch Ness? Why is it so hard to get an answer? One reason that it has been so difficult to prove the creature's existence is the size of Loch Ness. It is twenty-four miles long and a mile and a half wide at its widest point, making it the largest lake in the British Isles. It has an average depth of 450 feet, dropping to 900 feet in some places. The water is also very murky, making it difficult to take useful underwater photos. There are also dangerous currents in the loch, making an underwater search very risky.

Who: MOKÉLE-MBÊMBE

What: It is said to be a giant reptile with a long neck, about the size of an elephant. The skin is brownish gray and very smooth.
Where: The Likouala swamp region of the Congo in central Africa.
First recorded sighting: The leader of the Likouala Congo expedition of 1913–1914, Captain Freiherr von Stein zu Lausnitz, provided a detailed record of the Mokéle-Mbêmbe, as described to him by natives living in riverside villages. He concluded that the creature was a living dinosaur. Most scientists balked. After all, according to everything known about the natural world, all dinosaurs became extinct millions of years ago.
Recent findings: In 1980, Roy P. Mackal, a biochemist, led a group of explorers into the jungles of Africa in search of the elusive dinosaur. Many people in various isolated villages, miles apart, claimed they had seen it, and their descriptions matched exactly.
Verdict of science: Although the researchers on the 1980 expedition found no physical evidence, they concluded that the creature is indeed a small sauropod dinosaur, a creature that was supposed to have been extinct for more than 60 million years.

Who: GIANT OCTOPUS (KRAKEN)

What: The biggest known octopi weigh no more than 125 pounds, yet the elusive giant octopus is estimated to weigh at least five tons! Furthermore, the largest octopi known to science have tentacles ten to twelve feet long. The kraken, according to legend, has tentacles up to 100 feet long—long enough to grab a ship and strong enough to pull it under water.

Where: Legends of the kraken abound in Norway and Scandinavia. Similar creatures have been reported in the western Bahamas and other island nations. Cryptozoologists assume that if these creatures do exist, they live in the deepest parts of the ocean.

First recorded sighting: After a terrible winter storm in 1896 in St. Augustine, Florida, two children riding bicycles along the beach saw a huge, pink, glistening mass on the sand. Dr. DeWitt Webb, a local authority on sea life, came to see it for himself. Webb began digging around in the sand around the carcass and found two ragged tentacles. He estimated one of them to be more than sixty feet long! Webb arranged for a team of horses to pull the remains farther up the beach the next morning. Unfortunately another storm washed the carcass out to sea, and it was lost forever. Luckily, Webb had taken a tissue sample from the mass.

Verdict of science: In 1896, scientists dismissed the tissue sample as "whale blubber" without even examining it. It wasn't until 1956, when a marine biologist named Forrest Glen Wood came across the still-preserved tissue sample, that it was finally analyzed. Wood stated that although the sample was quite decomposed, it showed a remarkable similarity to octopus tissue. In fact, he said, it was more likely that it came from an octopus than a whale. Although this didn't prove the existence of the giant octopus, it strengthened the case for it.

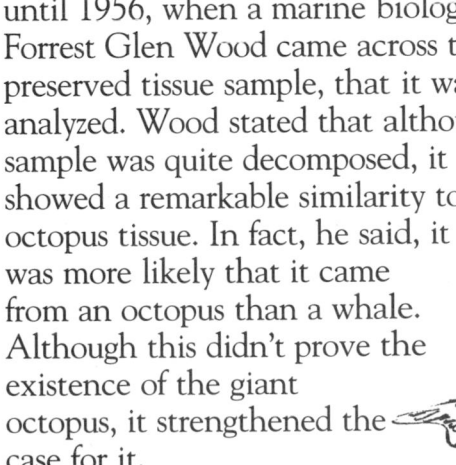

All Creatures Deadly & Dangerous

This animal is very bad; when attacked it defends itself.
—Anonymous, c. 1828

Science hasn't made up its mind about the creatures in the previous section. Bizarre and mysterious, deadly or friendly, the one question that remains to be answered is: Do they exist, or what? But the following creatures absolutely do exist, and there's no doubt about their scariness. Check out these creepy critters:

Venomous Spiders

Almost all spiders release a poison, a nerve toxin, from their fangs when they clamp down on a victim. While most spider venoms do not affect humans, there are exceptions. These spiders' bites can cause intense pain, paralysis, and sometimes even death:

Where	Spider
North America	Black widow
North America	Brown recluse
Australia	Burrowing tarantula
North America	Sac spider
Southern Brazil	Wolf spider

Killer Snakes

Many people fear snakes, and in some cases rightly so: some can be deadly. There are 200 kinds of snakes whose bite can kill people. These snakes inject their venom into their victims, sometimes causing permanent injury or even death. Snakes don't always release venom during a bite, however. Two usual warning signs that a snake *has* injected venom are sharp pain and swelling of the bitten area.

Watch out for these reptiles, some of the deadliest snakes in the grass:

Where	Snake
Europe	Asp viper
Southern and central Africa	Black mamba
African savannas	Boomslang
Asia	Braided krait
Southeast Asia	King cobra
North America	Northern copperhead
India to Africa (in dry areas)	Saw-scaled viper
Australia, New Guinea	Taipan
Australia	Tiger snake
North America	Western cottonmouth moccasin
North America	Western diamondback rattlesnake

DEADLY WATER CREATURES

Most bodies of water teem with life, some of it mysterious, some of it deadly—all of it beautiful. Think of these denizens of the deep the next time you spend a day at the shore.

GREAT WHITE SHARK:
The great white, which may grow to twenty-five feet, has attacked seals, large fish, and occasionally humans. Its sharp teeth have long cutting edges for ripping and tearing.

PIRANHA: These freshwater flesh eaters can grow to be eighteen inches long, with huge jaws and razor-sharp teeth. When they attack in a group, they can devour any warm-blooded creature— including a human—in minutes, leaving nothing behind but a skeleton.

MEAT-EATING PLANTS

While most plants receive all the nutrients they need from sunlight and soil, other plants just aren't satisfied unless they have a real meal. These meat-eating plants catch and eat insects and other small animals, such as frogs, squirrels, and even rabbits. Parents may be well advised to watch their small children closely near these plants!

SLOBBERING PINE: The slobbering pine is not a pine tree at all, but a plant with tall stalks covered with gooey liquid that traps struggling insects. Insects, weighted down by the liquid, fall down the stalk to the center of the plant, where they are liquefied and then absorbed.

BYBLIS: Similar in appearance and killing technique to the slobbering pine, these native Australian plants grow together in large, deadly clumps. They not only catch and digest insects but also feed on lizards, and even frogs, rabbits, and squirrels!

VENUS'S-FLYTRAP: Discovered in 1760, this unusual specimen is native to North Carolina. The leaves of the plant are shaped like jaws with jagged teeth, with hair triggers on each side. If an insect brushes against

Have Rats Gotten a Bad Rap?

Rats have been man's enemy throughout history—destroying crops, food in storage, and even live poultry. Today they still cause damage to the food industry—millions of dollars worth each year! Just the sight of them scares people silly. But rats are not inherently bad animals. As anyone with a domesticated rat companion can tell you, rats are meticulously clean and very intelligent. The reason rats are so abundant in our cities is that we leave so much garbage around for them to eat. Perhaps the scariest rats in history were the ones that helped to spread the bubonic plague, or Black Death, in the fourteenth century. Fleas living on infected rats bit people, giving them the sickness. In a few short years, one quarter of the population of Europe, nearly 25 million people, died of the plague.

one of the triggers only once, nothing will happen. An insect must brush against the hairs a *second* time to trigger the flytrap's nerve impulses and cause the leaves of the trap to shut. The flytrap tightens its grip—eventually shutting completely—and fills with liquid, drowning its helpless victim.

BLOOD SUCKERS

"The blood is the life," said Renfield, Dracula's ghoulish ally in Bram Stoker's *Dracula*. Apparently, the following creatures agree because blood is what they live on.

VAMPIRE BATS: Most bats feed on insects. The vampire bat, however, feeds on the blood of cattle and sometimes humans! It is a small bat, only about three inches long. Its fangs are so sharp and fine that the bat can insert them through the skin of its victim and into a vein without waking the meal provider. The bite causes the victim to bleed, and then the bat laps up the blood from the skin.

LEECHES: These slimy worms have suckers at each end of their body, one for attaching to an animal's body, the other for drinking blood. Most live in the water. Some can grow to seventeen inches long. Others are so small they may be swallowed when drinking river water; these leeches can cling inside the throat, causing terrible pain and sometimes death. Land leeches, however, found on the islands of the Pacific, are the ones feared most. If a leech enters a sleeping person's nose to feed on blood, it will become so fat with blood that it can't get out again, suffocating its victim!

SHEER FEAR

When something in this world scares us, whether it's a real threat, a superstition, or a phobia, our bodies spring into action. From the sweat under our arms to the confusing images of a nightmare, our bodies are finding ways to manage our fear.

FAR-OUT PHOBIAS

"The only thing we have to fear is fear itself."

—Franklin D. Roosevelt, First Inaugural Address

A phobia is an intense but irrational fear. During a phobic attack the body reacts as if it is facing a real threat, even though the fear may be about something as harmless as clouds or dolls. Read through this list and see how many phobias you have.

FEAR OF FEAR IS PHOBOPHOBIA!

FAR-OUT PHOBIAS

If you are afraid of . . .	then you have . . .
beards	pogonophobia
being happy	cherophobia
books	bibliophobia
cemeteries	coimetrophobia
chickens	alektorophobia
clothes	vestiphobia
clouds	nephophobia
dancing	chorophobia
dinner conversation	deipnophobia
dolls (especially of dolls staring at you)	pediophobia
flowers	anthophobia
flutes (both the instrument and the sound it makes)	aulophobia
girls	parthenophobia
going to school	scolionophobia
hair (seeing it, or having your own touched)	trichophobia
handwriting	graphophobia
laughter	geliophobia
mirrors	catoptrophobia
money (especially the germs that are on it)	chrematophobia
numbers	numerophobia
peanut butter sticking to the roof of your mouth	arachibutyrophobia
relatives	syngenesophobia
rust	iophobia
spiders	arachnophobia
string	linonophobia
teeth	odonophobia
tests	testophobia
thirteen, the number	triskaidekaphobia
vegetables	lachanophobia

Watch Out! It's a . . . 13!!

The fear of the number 13 dates back thousands of years. While the true origins of this fear are lost to history, today the fear of the number 13 is so widespread that most office buildings and large hotels don't have a thirteenth floor. The buttons on the elevator will jump from 12 to 14 (as if the people staying on the "14th floor" don't know they're really on the 13th!).

SU·SU·SU· SUPERSTITIONS

Superstition is the poetry of life.
—Goethe

Studies show that people are as superstitious today as they have ever been. But why? Why do people believe that knocking on wood or avoiding black cats will affect their fate? Some social scientists say that superstitions are a way for people to cope with anxiety and fear in an unpredictable world. But maybe superstitions are not "coping mechanisms" after all; perhaps they are instinctive laws of nature that should not be ignored—except at our peril ...

POPULAR SUPERSTITIONS

Below you will find some of the most popular superstitions to have creeped into our culture—leaving wary believers forever on the lookout.

BLACK CATS: In America, many people fear that they will have bad luck if a black cat crosses their path. In England, however, they get worried if a *white* cat crosses their path.

LADDERS: It is considered very unlucky to walk under a ladder. If there is no way to walk around it, cross your fingers while walking under the ladder and keep them crossed until you see a dog.

MIRRORS: You will have seven years of bad luck for breaking a mirror. Why? People used to believe that a mirror reflected not just the image but the soul of a person. If the mirror were broken, the soul would also be broken. It would apparently take seven years to pull itself back together.

UMBRELLAS: It is very unlucky to open an umbrella in the house. Some people think it will bring misfortune to the entire household; others think that the person who opened it will die before the year is out.

THE EVIL EYE: One of the oldest superstitions is the belief in the evil eye—the conviction that some people have the power to cause death or illness with a glance. The oldest reference to the evil eye dates back to 3000 B.C.—nearly 5,000 years ago.

Some people may be born with this awful power and not know they have it. Other people may spend years trying to develop in themselves the power of the evil eye. Over the centuries, people have sought ways to protect themselves from its dark influence. Even today, in parts of Europe, Mexico, and Central America, people still take steps to protect themselves from the evil eye.

How to Protect Yourself from the Evil Eye

Two small amulets that originated in Italy are thought to be powerful antidotes: the *mano cornuta,* in the shape of a curved horn; and the *fig,* in the shape of a fist with the thumb between the second and middle finger of the hand.

Other protective items are bells, red ribbons, red coral, shamrocks (four-leafed clovers), and designs in the shape of eyes. Strong smells are also powerful protectors; in Greece simply saying *skordtho* (the Greek word for "garlic") is enough.

If you are caught off guard and you believe someone has cast an evil eye upon you, you can still protect yourself if you immediately spit or make the shape of the *còrno* or *fig* with your hand.

mano cornuta

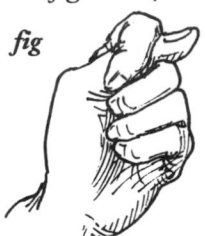

fig

NASTY NIGHTMARES

I will show you fear in a handful of dust.

—T. S. Eliot,

"The Waste Land"

Dreams of death and destruction, monsters and ghouls. Everyone has the occasional nightmare, but about one in twelve people suffer from them regularly. Where do nightmares come from? What causes them? And how can you make them go away?

Sleep researchers generally agree that people who have many nightmares are revealing in their dreams things they are afraid of while awake, but these fears are usually cloaked in symbolic form. Nightmares may occur after a traumatic incident and be a way of playing out the stress caused by the trauma. If nightmares happen again and again, they may be a sign of deeper emotional conflicts.

Luckily there is help for people who suffer from recurrent nightmares or night terrors. Sleep therapists have devised many strategies to reduce or eliminate nightmares.

ARE YOU PRONE TO NIGHTMARES?

Although anyone may experience the occasional nightmare, sleep researchers have come up with a nightmare "type"—people who are more prone than others to have regular nightmares. Do any of the following characteristics apply to you?

Do you:	Are you:
• Feel like an outsider? a rebel?	• Sensitive?
• Feel like you're different from other people?	• Creative?
• Drift easily into daydreams?	• Emotional?
	• Vulnerable (open to others)?
	• Empathetic (able to feel what others are feeling)?
	• Artistic?

If you answered yes to many of these questions, you are more likely than others to have nightmares.

HOW TO MAKE YOUR NIGHTMARES GO AWAY

The following seven techniques may help banish nightmares:

1. Establish a nighttime routine and follow it every night as you get ready to go to bed. If you can unwind and relax before going to sleep, you won't be as likely to have a nightmare.

2. If you wake up from a nightmare in the middle of the night, take a deep breath, try to calm down, and then go back to sleep and try to change the dream's ending.

3. Be aware that dreams are a normal part of sleep, and nightmares are a normal part of dreaming. Remind yourself that they can't really hurt you.

4. If you can't remember the details of your dream the next morning, don't force yourself to; this will only increase the stress. But if you do remember your dream, feel free to talk about it and get the feelings out.

5. Try to determine what your nightmare is trying to tell you. Usually it is your mind's own way of revealing problems or worries you have during the day. If you can use your nightmare to get clues to your waking state, and then resolve or discuss those real problems, your nightmares about them will go away.

6. Replay the dream in your mind while you are awake and feel safe. Replay it again and again in as much vivid detail as you can remember. This is called "desensitization." If you face the scary image enough times, it will become less scary and eventually go away.

7. Practice the technique of "lucid dreaming." This is a state of being aware that you are dreaming while you are still in the dream, and of being able to control what occurs in the dream. There are many books available on the subject. It takes a lot of practice, however, and not everyone can learn how to do it, but it may be worth a try.

THE PHYSIOLOGY OF FEAR

It made our hair stand up in panic fear.

—Sophocles, 406 B.C.

Fear is a normal and useful emotion. When a threat is real, fear can cause you to take quick action, fight, or run away. Sometimes the feelings of fright may be scary in themselves if you don't know what is happening to you. Look at this diagram to see what can happen to your body when you are frightened!

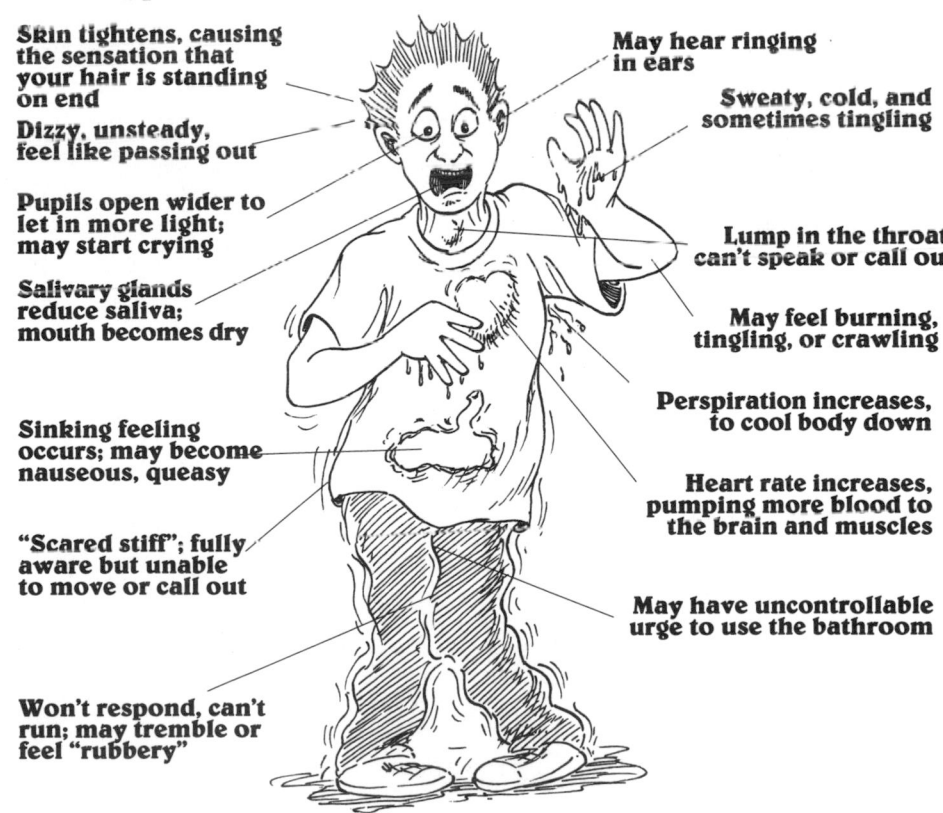

Skin tightens, causing the sensation that your hair is standing on end

Dizzy, unsteady, feel like passing out

Pupils open wider to let in more light; may start crying

Salivary glands reduce saliva; mouth becomes dry

Sinking feeling occurs; may become nauseous, queasy

"Scared stiff"; fully aware but unable to move or call out

Won't respond, can't run; may tremble or feel "rubbery"

May hear ringing in ears

Sweaty, cold, and sometimes tingling

Lump in the throat; can't speak or call out

May feel burning, tingling, or crawling

Perspiration increases, to cool body down

Heart rate increases, pumping more blood to the brain and muscles

May have uncontrollable urge to use the bathroom

INDEX